CW00556132

Yellow Slicker

Deanna Nese

Green Avenue Books & Publishing LLC

First Edition Printing, January 2023

ISBN : 9798218074838

Ebook Edition

ISBN : 9798218074845

Green Avenue Books & Publishing, LLC

Printed in the U.S.A.

This is for Sam, Dylan, and Clara with all my love.

1995

I WAS MALCONTENT, DISTRACTED, and full of Chinese food and beer. It was Saturday, June 10, 1995. I'd left the gathering of my friends in a huff, not that anyone noticed, and took the long route home. I knew it by heart, the sharp turns and the possibility of encountering wildlife, a roaming coyote or deer.

Martin's girlfriend, Jane, had contacted us, the old crew from high school. She was staying at her parents' house for the weekend and we were all invited to join her, sort of like a last goodbye to our youth before taking on the roles of responsible adults. All of us were staying in town for the summer, most having just graduated college, but before setting off to tackle life. Hudson and I, the only two non-college grads, had just opened the comic store, so the gathering, besides being a reunion, was celebratory. There was no date for me. I was unattached. At 22, I had already let my appearance go. I'd grown thick and soft around the middle and my skin was ruddy, but not in a handsome way. That very morning, I noticed my hairline looked farther back than it should for a guy my age. I was still a kid, but I didn't look like one, didn't feel like one.

Now when I flip through pictures from that night. I see I was depressed, maybe even in a crisis. The slicked back hair that was too long, too scraggly, the shadows under the eyes, the mouth in a straight line in every shot, untucked shirt, awful baggy khakis. What a mess I was. I felt alone and wanted to be alone. I stepped outside to get away from my friends.

On the perch from the upper balcony, I stared out into the quiet darkness at the estates below. There were few lights, and the fog that settled nightly diffused them. Moist air mixed with sea salt with underpinnings of horses and damp hay. It was a scent I never grew tired of. I heard the sounds of laughter and hollering from inside and when I entered, shutting the French doors behind me, I learned that Martin and Jane would be the first of our friends to get married. I offered my congratulations, while in my head I told myself they were fools. *Who in their right mind would make a lifetime commitment so young?* At this point, I still hadn't had a proper relationship, unless you count Karen, from high school, who promptly broke it off in 11th grade as soon as I wrecked my car. She wouldn't be seen in the old Honda.

I threaded past the group and proceeded to the service porch with the overflowing trash can of takeout Chinese delivery boxes, grabbed myself a fortune cookie, and snuck out to the front of the house. My sneakers crunched on the gravel driveway, and it occurred to me how pretentious this driveway, this house, this whole town was, including the friends I'd just abandoned. I can't say why my eyes were stinging or why the tears fell and splashed on my pants while I sat in my car and collected my thoughts. I breathed in and out, counting to ten, knowing I needed to leave soon or someone might find me and not let me go, or ask me to explain the state I was in. My skin flushed with renewed embarrassment as I recalled our earlier conversation.

"So, you think you'll actually follow through with the comic shop, Dunc?" Martin asked. "Or will you abandon it like every other project you start?" June added.

"He better not! I put in ten thousand. I even had to take a loan, not like 'rich boy' over here whose parents just write him checks," Hudson said.

Though they were only joking, it was only some light-hearted ribbing; I felt exposed and out of place. The words were cutting and held too much truth.

Our crew had the house for the entire weekend. Everyone was meant to stay and make pancakes in the morning, nurse hangovers with Bloody Marys, swim, lie around, maybe ride the horses. I couldn't. I needed to leave. I've replayed it a thousand times, and in the re-play version, I always stay. I join the party, congratulate Martin and Jane, and even strike up a romance with Joelle, whom I always cared for and who was also single that night. Instead, I left.

It was the third curvy turn. One hand was on the wheel, the other fumbling with the wrapper of the fortune cookie. There was only darkness and a light, misty drizzle. I hadn't seen a single other car. I felt fine; the beers had settled in, the Jello shots, too. Combined with all those greasy Chinese dishes, I absolutely had to be sober by then. I glanced down for a second, a split second, then I felt the thud, the sickening, crunching thud. My body whipped back with the force of it. Pain shot through my neck as the seatbelt dug in. My eye caught a flash of bright yellow, then nothing. I kept driving, not breaking my pace of about 25 to 30 miles an hour, and then I pulled over to process what had just happened.

No one walked this road even in the daytime. It was far too dangerous. There was no shoulder, just a low guardrail where the drop-off was steep, and on the other side, the mountain or sometimes a steep road leading to another estate. No way I hit a person, impossible, just no. But what was the thud? I'd hit something. Maybe a deer or, God forbid, someone's pet. That would be beyond awful. I pulled over and put on the hazards, then thought better of it, and extinguished them quickly. What if someone saw me? What if a private security truck happened by? I did not need to explain what I was doing on the side of the road in the rain at 1:35 AM to some rent-a-cop with an attitude. Had I skidded, left a mark? Would the thing have fallen over the side and down the hill? How steep was it there? I needed to go back and look. By then it was raining steadily. I was definitely sober if I hadn't been before. I continued past my parents' house and circled back. I knew there was a shoulder near where whatever just happened, happened. I would stop there, get my mag light from the trunk and check out the scene, just to be safe.

I parked and turned off the lights. I'd still not encountered a single other vehicle. I got out and walked in the rain, thinking only fleetingly of my safety if someone should come hurtling drunk down the road. They'd never expect me. I'd never know what hit me. It was sobering to realize I didn't really care; I was numb. I don't know what I expected to see, but I saw nothing.

No fresh skid marks, though it'd be hard to tell in the rain and not knowing a precise location. I kept shining my light down the side of the hill, maybe expecting to find some broken branches or a hurt and dying animal. I only saw the squashed skunk next to the guardrail that still smelled a little after being there for at least the last two weeks. Poor guy. Sure, so maybe I'd hit a skunk and the poor thing had been flung to the side and down the hill and into the ravine. Maybe I'd hit nothing and imagined this whole thing and was truly losing it. I should have stayed with my friends. Every day from that day on, that thought would echo and plague me.

I got back to my car and drove home, took a shower, and got into my bed. At no point did I consider calling the police. There was nothing to report. Sleep eluded me. Thoughts of how I'd spent my life thus far invaded my mind. Not usually introspective, it was remarkable how little attention I paid to myself or my future, what I wanted. My diagnosis of Attention Deficit Disorder came early in my school days and provided a convenient pass not to focus, and I was glad for it. Mediocrity was comfortable. It made me fun, the good-time guy, a blast to hang out with, but nothing more. People didn't ask me for personal thoughts or opinions on anything of substance. Yet, now I was responsible for a business, and was possibly a wanted criminal who fled a crime scene. Would my parents come to my rescue this time?

Pushing the thought of the accident out of my consciousness, I focused instead on the comic shop. I was positive the storefront was a mistake. It literally began as a conversation during a stop while Hudson and I were mountain biking. We were stupid. Neither of us had a clue how to open and run a business, what it would take, but we came up with ten thousand dollars each, Hudson from working two jobs, saving every penny and getting a small loan, and me, as he pointed out, from asking my parents for a check, which they wrote out, no questions asked, always happy to support me. We chose a prime location downtown and set up our comic store with no market research or solid business plan, just a love for comics and the idea that it would be 'fun.' The few stragglers who wandered in took a quick look around and quickly left. On day one, no one bought a single item from Knight's Comics. Not one. It was a soft opening, but I knew with total frightening certainty; it indicated not a prosperous endeavor, but a dead end. My thoughts raced, and I formulated a way out of the newly opened store that bore my name, rehearsing the conversation I needed to have with Hudson, and knowing how angry and disappointed he'd be.

The next day was Sunday, and the comic store was closed. I slept till 10, woke up in tangled sheets that smelled sour and needed a wash, then strolled past the pool over to the main house where my parents lived, trying to push the events of the previous night out of my mind. I never kept food in the guest house, I just helped myself to my parents' pantry and fridge. I grabbed a jar of peanut butter and a half-eaten loaf of bread and began to mindlessly construct a sandwich. There was leftover coffee in the percolator, and I poured a mug of the black and bitter stuff. My dad sat on the counter stool dressed in gray slacks and a short sleeve chambray button-down shirt, hair slicked back, smelling of aftershave. He gave me a sideways glance, looking over his half glasses, and a "Good morning, Duncan." He was finishing reading the newspaper and waiting for my mom to be ready to leave for church. Did I want to go?

"Nah, not today, but thanks Dad, say a prayer for me."

This, or a similar version of the conversation, took place every Sunday. Then I changed my mind. "You know what, Dad? I'll come along."

I went. Nothing changed at St. Mark's Catholic Church. I recited all the prayers and responses automatically, even though it had been a long time for me. The hard wooden pew with the worn-off varnish, and the smell of the missalette, were so familiar. Halfway through the service, I replayed the events of the night before, now positive I must have imagined it or dreamt it. If I'd hit a person, there would be a huge dent in the front of my car, surely, but there was no way I actually hit someone. It wasn't possible. I begged off brunch and asked, "Would you mind just dropping me back home?" My parents obliged.

I approached my car with a lot of self-talk. *I'll just look and put the whole thing to rest. It was nothing, nothing. It could not have happened.* In last night's haste, I'd pulled the front of the car up close to the wall of the guest house. The right side was practically wedged into the decorative bushes, and I took a deep inhalation of star jasmine. I wasn't concerned with keeping my car nice. The entire body was covered in dents and pockmarks. I didn't care. Having a nice car was never a thing for me. That's what I like to tell myself since it was my only option after I wrecked the car I was given for my 16th birthday. My parents made me get a part-time job and drive an old car to teach me "responsibility". I needed to back it up in order to fully inspect the front, so I did. The right front bumper had a sizable dent that I was about 80% sure was new.

What would create a dent like that? I crouched down in the gravel to get a closer look and I saw a smudge of yellow. I licked my finger and rubbed at it; it peeled off in tiny rolls. Caught on the underside of the bumper was a small piece of yellow rubberized fabric, the kind a raincoat would be made of, like the one the crossing guard lady who held up traffic each morning at the bottom of the hill because she clearly has an attitude problem, wears. Just like that. I breathed deeply.

Did I run into the crossing guard lady at one in the morning as she was wandering aimlessly in the rain? Is she unconscious right now, or dead? No way.

I pinched the fabric in my fingers and pulled it free from underneath the bumper. The edges were rough as if it was torn from something bigger. *Was this evidence?* I went inside to my room, stashed it in the corner of my sock drawer, sat on my bed for a moment, and tried to figure out what to do. The crew was probably enjoying pancakes and may, or may not, have even noticed I wasn't there. I wondered, should I call the police and make a report? I couldn't. I'd sound nuts, and what if I was guilty? Last year, I spent a day in jail for multiple unpaid parking tickets. When I was booked in, a fat, greasy-haired guard collected my shoelaces. So I wouldn't hang myself. I told myself it wasn't embarrassing at all when my dad picked me up. He paid the fine I owed, said nothing, and never even asked for the money back. It was worse than being yelled at and chastised. I felt like he expected this from me.

Too keyed up to stay home, I returned to the house where my friends were. As I suspected, they were just rousing from sleep, nursing Bloody Marys, and waiting for the pizza delivery guy. Turns out no one was in a condition to make pancakes after the night of partying.

My explanation was ready should I need it. I went home to sleep in my own bed. My back was hurting, but no one asked where I'd been. It wasn't clear if they knew I was gone at all. That moment was the most isolated I have ever felt. I didn't belong. I never had. They could be sitting here with a murderer for all they knew. I hung out for a while. I stepped out to the back deck where there was a decent view of the road if I looked to the left. With binoculars I found in the house, I scanned the road and hillside. Nothing. See, nothing happened, I rationalized. The yellow scrap and dent? Who knows how they got there? I ate a couple slices of pizza and took off soon after, making up an excuse of a brewing migraine, totally plausible. Everyone knew I had them regularly.

The next day I woke up early, Monday. My plan was to see if the crossing guard was on duty. As I drove, I became more and more worried that I wouldn't see her in her usual spot. She might be ill, or she easily could have retired. It's June though, kids are out of school, so she will for sure not be there, I reasoned. But, she was, in her bright yellow jacket and smudged glasses, sitting in her director's chair, ready to pop up and hold high her sign, causing traffic to back up for half a mile while she waddled into the road. Summer school. So I didn't kill her. My shoulders relaxed slightly, my perspiration turned to chilly beads in every pore of my back. I wished I could feel more relief than I did.

Next, I stopped in at the comic shop and broke the news to Hudson; I wanted out. The comic shop venture was a mistake.

"Look Hud, you know I'd make a horrible partner. You know how unreliable I am. You'd be much better off with a guy who knows how to run a successful business, someone who actually cares."

"Bro, that's low. So now, after all, we've put into this, you're bailing on me? Unbelievable. You are a grade-A asshole, Duncan. And I may not forgive you. Ever."

"I know, and I would deserve it. I get it. But I'm pretty sure you can find another investor. I won't just leave you hanging. We just need to find another investor. Simple. Then you can buy me out."

"Oh, and I'll be keeping the name, so don't even think of asking me to change it."

"No, I definitely wouldn't. Knight's Comics is a perfect name."

Not surprisingly, it didn't take long for Hudson to find another investor. I was relieved and fine with the fact that I was quitting without ever really trying. I went home and holed up. I slept. A lot. More than was healthy for anyone. Often staying in bed for over 14 hours at a stretch, getting up for food or to use the bathroom, and to let my parents know I was still alive. And then I woke up. If I had hurt, damaged, or killed someone, then I should at least be grateful to A. be alive, and B. not get caught.

1996

Today I drove down the hill for a singular purpose. I had an idea that would not let go, an image of a brown leather-bound book with blank pages. When I get an image, I need to honor it. It's there for a reason and this seemed harmless enough. Anything to rid myself of the too frequently occurring memory of the yellow flash in the night, as I now think of it. I headed to the Village Book Shoppe. It's a favorite of mine. Half of the store is outside under some precariously crafted overhangs with back-to-back book shelves. If the store's not open, you are directed by a paper sign thumb tacked to the shelf to read the price and deposit the money in the metal lock box or bring it the next time you come. And people do. The inside is musty and charming, as a bookshop should be. The newer books are organized and alphabetized, but the old treasures are everywhere. There are first editions in glass cases. It's not wise to visit with something in mind, better to wander and see what you find and leave with something you didn't know you needed.

The Village Book Shoppe is a beloved fixture of Ocean View Village.

"Where can I find a journal?"

The bored and barefoot girl side-eyed me and waved her skinny tattooed arm in the general direction of the west wall of books. Fine. Super helpful, nose-ring girl. I picked up a pink Hello Kitty diary with a broken lock and some pages filled in.

Today was a BORING day!!! We had inside recess and Ryan did not choose me for Heads Up Seven Up. He would not even look at me. Bad day.

I felt a little voyerish, but I read on. It was the only thing resembling a journal, after all. Jenna, her name was written on the front, must have outgrown it or realized it's never safe to write down your feelings. Someone could see them. I envisioned her now as an older college girl, a sad girl, miserable with her life and quietly planning her own suicide, and I shuddered. I tried to send a positive, encouraging message to her through the universe.

No, take it from someone who might have killed someone. Stay alive!, I thought, and returned the pink diary to the shelves. It was not the right fit for me. I kept looking through the shelves, and there it was. The exact journal I pictured with just a few pages torn from the front and a watermark on the cover where the previous owner had plonked a sweaty glass. I thumbed the pages, and all were beautifully blank-inviting my thoughts. Written on the last page was, "The End" in a curlicue cursive and I loved it. I would keep it. It was fitting for the last page.

I purchased the leather journal, took it home, and on the inside cover, I wrote my name, then documented everything from the night of June 10, 1995, and my thoughts about it. I figured it would help me move on. Process, and move on. I felt really good, to be honest. I used to keep a journal when I was a kid, but never kept up with the entries, kind of like "Jenna" of the Hello Kitty journal. I wonder whatever happened to those writings from my youth? Maybe my mom kept them, or maybe I tossed them when I was weeding through my old belongings.

June marked the one-year anniversary of the incident. Over this past year, my obsessive daily walks/hikes to the site and surrounding area became weekly, then biweekly, then whenever. The ravine is fully overgrown now and no reasonable person could safely go down. I never actually did. But I looked very carefully all around and saw nothing. I'd continued to drive my old car, but eventually relented and agreed to let my parents buy me a new one. I would need something decent if I was going to show properties.

Right, so I forgot to mention that after waking up out of my months-long stupor, and weaseling out of the comic store venture, I needed a plan. I decided to attend classes to get my real estate license. So after ten weeks of applying myself to the task, I was a newly minted real estate agent, and ready to sell. I'd always been fascinated with properties. I loved seeing the inside of houses and how people lived and figured I could be convincing and with these traits; I believed I could, and would, do well in the profession.

After finishing my courses and passing the exam, I inquired at Village Real Estate to see if they were hiring and I was accepted immediately. Which really meant they had an available office space that I could rent for $650/month and be a part of their team, plus pay them a percentage of any sales I made. I'd get my own business cards, that I paid for of course, and access to the MLS which allowed me to see all of the listed and recently sold properties in the tri-county area. There was no salary, but loads of potential. A look at the vehicles in the parking lot led me to believe my new colleagues were in fact quite successful. It was all up to me. I was ready to go with modern office furniture, a luxury car, newly printed business cards (Village Real Estate: Duncan Knight, Realtor), and a custom tailored wardrobe all thanks once again to my parents' generosity.

No one wanted my old car, not even for parts. My metallic blue dinged and dented up Honda Accord had served me well, but it was time. First, I pried off the old blue and gold California license plates. Next, I drove it to a junkyard and paid the lot owner a hundred bucks to keep it. And then I briefly got sentimental and said I needed a minute alone. He gave me a knowing look and encouraged me to take my time, to take as long as I needed. I approached my old and faithful buddy with nostalgia, recalling how some of the dents were earned. Two friends jumping on the hood not two weeks after I got the car caused it to be permanently caved in. The passenger door had a large one from putting the car in reverse while it was open and almost taking the entire door off. Then there was the time I wedged it next to a rural mailbox resulting in a long dent and scratched off paint. I rubbed my hands over that dent, used a fingernail to scrape off a chip of long-faded navy blue paint, and then got inside and took one last look inside the glove box and center console. I reached under the seat and fetched out an intact fortune cookie, perfectly preserved in a clear wrapper, with the little white paper sticking out. Holy crap. This was my fortune from the night. Gingerly, I put it in my windbreaker pocket, walked back to the guy, and gave him his money. My dad had followed me in his car, so I got in.

"That was hard," I told him. "Me and that piece of shit have really been through a lot." He just nodded in his quiet way, patted my knee twice, and drove us home.

Alone. I needed to be alone. I went straight to the pool house. I closed the drapes over the glass doors, as if someone would look in. I sat at my desk, set the cookie down on my large calendar ink blotter, and stared at it as if it somehow held an answer. Finally, I broke it apart and pulled out the paper. The red writing said, "Tonight you will experience a life-changing event." I reasoned that if I didn't eat the cookie, the fortune would not come true. I rolled the fortune paper into the tiniest possible cylinder and put it in my sock drawer next to the scrap of yellow. I flushed the cookie down the toilet.

1997

T HIS HAS BEEN A year to take personal inventory. I am
here and there must be a reason. If someone lost their
life because of me, then I shouldn't squander whatever is left
of mine. I've made some profound decisions. Decision 1: I
am not moving out of my parents' house. The estate is huge
and I am their only child so there is truly no point. Anyhow,
the pool house, which I have to myself, is just as if I have my
own place. I know little birdies should fly the nest, but this
bird is staying put. Also, I've really started to get to know
my parents and there is no one else I trust to look after them
when the time comes, and they want me to stay, and I love
them for that. They have never asked anything of me, and
in my younger years, I was an unappreciative, spoiled brat.
Anything I wanted to do, they supported, but I never really
took advantage of opportunities available to me. So, Decision
2: It's time to grow up, take responsibility. I've sold a couple
of properties, and since I have no real expenses, almost all of
my earnings go straight into the bank.

Have I done anything about the incident? No. Does it continue to plague me? Yes. Do I plan to confess? (if that's even the correct term, I mean I may not have even done anything wrong) No, not at this time. Writing down my memories with all the details of the night has helped me process the incident. I benefit from getting my thoughts on paper. It calms me. I've never been great with deep conversation and there is no one I can talk to about what troubles me. Who would understand? I couldn't take the judgment.

I'm starting to notice strange things and sometimes I wonder if I'm not actually a little crazy. I would never admit this to another human, but I feel as though I'm being watched. Like there was a witness to that night, that someone knows something. I realize it's impossible. I should just move on and enjoy my life, gotta stop being so damn paranoid.

As an extra precaution, against what I'm not certain, I've started to lock the pool house when I'm out. On two occasions I felt uneasy in my space. Once there was an unfamiliar scent in my room, like wet earth. The housekeeper does not clean the pool house, and it was not a day that either the gardening crew or the pool maintenance guy was scheduled, and yet, I smelled it, like the bank of a pond. The second time, I sensed that the air had been disturbed. It felt off. I checked to see if anything was moved and noticed my journal on the desk. I might have left it there, but the usual place I keep it is on the lower shelf of the nightstand. Both times I asked my parents if they'd been in. No, they had not. So I asked them for the key, and none of us could locate it because we never use it and it's not the same as the main house key. I called a locksmith, but canceled the appointment when I remembered the old hiding place.

On the left side of the garage, I found the key under a rock. I retrieved it, cleaned it, drove to the hardware shop in the village, and had a copy made. I confirmed that the new copy worked and returned the spare key to its hiding place, remembering back when the bus would drop me off from school down the road, and I'd let myself in while waiting for my parents to get home. That was when all the keys were the same and I wore mine on a lanyard around my neck. Dad hid an extra so none of us would ever find ourselves locked out. During one of the remodels, they re-keyed the main house locks, but the pool house lock was never changed. We have no close neighbors and the main door of the pool house has always been kept unlocked for the gardeners and the pool cleaner in case they needed to use the facilities, or wanted to grab a soda from the fridge. I certainly never cared before. I asked my parents to let the workers know they should use the restroom in the garage from now on, and that I would put a small fridge in there with sodas.

"Tell them I'm using the pool house as an office now and I can't be disturbed while I'm working. It's probably best anyway because sometimes I have a client's information on my desk and other sensitive papers. I'm sure they'll understand."

It's probably paranoia. But, because of my unease, I feel better taking precautions. I'll keep my journal hidden too. The last thing I need is for someone to read it.

1998

TWENTY-five. WHICH MEANS MY life is one quarter over,
if I should live to be 100. I haven't done too much I'm
proud of so far. Real estate sales are going well. If I'm honest,
it's thanks in large part to Mom and Dad. My business cards
are all over Dad's office and he recommends me to all his
clients. He's so firmly in my corner, it humbles me, and
I'm trying to accept it and not feel so unworthy. Mom is
quick to make trays of goodies for every Open House I host
and to talk me up to all of her friends. She spends hours in
the kitchen, her silver hair in a bun, blue apron on, making
cookies and finger sandwiches, veggies and dips, and mint
lemonade. She sets it all up in a beautiful arrangement with
little plates and napkins with my business cards in an acrylic
holder right next to it.

"You'll not find a more trustworthy, reliable, and honest
realtor than my Duncan. He's simply the best. I couldn't
be more proud of him. He'll get you the best deal too, and
he knows everyone around here. He's got the inside scoop.
Here, take some of his cards. Tell your friends."

Mom, my cheerleader. The majority of my leads come from her and Dad. They are so well-connected. It's true I have to close the deal, but without them, I don't know what my opportunities to do that would be, and now as friends tell friends, my client list grows as does my reputation. I'm known for being no nonsense and to the point- an agent who will work to get you a good deal, no matter if you're the buyer or the seller.

I was on my way home from looking at a property, a nice sprawling mid-century modern style with an amazing stone fireplace and I was thinking about how I would play up its features to my clients. The timeless quality, the symmetry of the open beams, the warmth, the views. *You don't see framed windows like this anymore. This garden, just waiting for your love and attention. These are mature avocado trees. Did you notice the seasonal stream out back? Yes, you could definitely bring your horses. It's zoned for livestock, too, if you want a gentleman's farm.*

The descriptions come so easily to me now. It just takes some careful listening, and I can convince a buyer that what I have is what they want. It's also what many other buyers want, so best to act fast. I'm fine with my strategies because my clients have the money; if they didn't, they couldn't afford to even look in this area. Also, I have the receptionist at the office do a pre-screen for a loan amount, so I know exactly what they can spend, then I suggest an offer just under that amount, but over the asking price to guarantee the acceptance of the seller, so they feel like they're getting a deal. Everyone wins.

I decided I would hike the trail to the waterfall, maybe even jump into the swimming hole if it was deep enough. I know the trail well and have traversed it numerous times since my youth. I could hike it from muscle memory. *It should be serene, middle of the morning, Wednesday, middle of the week.* I had thrown my shorts and daypack in the backseat of my Lexus and had slipped into one of the bedrooms to change before leaving the property listing. The few spots where you can parallel park by the trailhead were taken, so I doubled back and parked on the upper road's shoulder, and realizing I would have to pass "the place," I quickened my pace. A slight breeze pricked up the hairs on my arms and I caught a chill. The road is narrow here, but I still stopped and peered down into the ravine. I hadn't looked at it from this angle in a long time, but nevertheless I felt the familiar rush of anxiety. The entire canyon is thoroughly overgrown and dry. I envisioned someone tossing a dead body over the rail. It would crash through the bushes and rest somewhere on the hill, maybe catching on a branch of one of the trees that grew out from the side. The bushes would fold back into themselves and no one would ever see or suspect a thing. A body could be resting there right now in fact. Maybe even one that has been there for a couple of years. *Why do I do this to myself?* My reverie was interrupted when I heard something. I could hardly see down to the lower road and could not pinpoint the source of the sound. A yelping sound. There was no way I could ignore it. I called out several times, but received no response.

"Are you hurt? Can I help you?" Fully aware that it could be my mind playing tricks on me, and also knowing there wasn't a safe way to descend, I willed myself to keep walking to the trailhead and forget about it. I tried to enjoy the hike, come back to my senses, breathe the fresh air, but could only focus on the sounds I'd heard. Two teen boys came up from behind, then passed me on the trail. I caught a snippet of their conversation.

"Let's go up to the old guy's house and find the hangout everyone's always talking about."

"Ok, I think it's like a goat stable with a fence around it."

This meant they would take the left fork of the trail, not the right to the waterfall, so I might get the falls to myself today, unless someone was already there. Then I remembered the other cars and figured it was not probable. Too many people have discovered this trail in the last few years. It's no longer a secret known only to locals.

"Yeah, my brother goes up there and parties with his friends sometimes."

"Maybe they left some beer."

"We gotta be careful though, the old guy's got a gun."

I smiled to myself. They were heading up to the same old shed we used to go to in high school. Some things never change. The old man must be ancient by now. I had never seen him, only heard him cursing, saying we should stay the hell off his property, or he'd shoot us. Part of me wanted to follow the boys, but I kept thinking about the noise I heard, so I cut my hike short and headed back to the trailhead.

When I reached my car, I drove down to the lower road to see if I could find anything there, hoping to put my mind at ease. I parked by the entrance to the fire road and began calling out. I heard the yelping again and knew it must be a dog. I could have called Animal Control and let them deal with it. I searched in the bushes for almost an hour, the yelps turning to soft whimpers, and then I found him.

It was June 10, 1:35pm, exactly 3 years and 12 hours from the time of the incident. He wasn't able to walk, was cut up and in terrible shape. Dried mud clung to his patchy fur. He looked at me with soulful, deep brown eyes. He was relieved to see me. I carried him out of the brush and into the brighter daylight. He was a yellow lab and made me think of *Old Yeller*. I took him to my car and laid out a blanket from my trunk on the back seat for him. I drove straight to the veterinarian in the village. When we arrived, the technician took him to the back right away, and they started an IV to get him fluids. The vet surmised he was approximately a year old based on his bone size and his teeth. Dr. Darnel was kind. I could tell how much she loved animals.

"You saved him just in time. He can't walk because he's so malnourished and dehydrated. He probably would have died within the hour. But there are no major injuries, nothing broken." I had saved him just in time. She gave him his vaccines, assuring me it would not harm him if he'd already gotten them. She also gave him a shot of antibiotics and sold me some high-calorie food to get him back in shape.

"Keep him calm and comfortable. I think he's going to be okay."

"Absolutely," I said, and, "Thank you."

"I'd like to see him again in a week," she said, "sooner if he doesn't seem to improve."

"I hope I'll be able to keep him," I replied, truly hoping I would.

There were no signs posted around the village for a lost dog. I reluctantly, but dutifully, advertised him as "found" in the Village Reporter and visited the local rescue shelter to see if anyone was looking for him there. After two weeks, I crossed my fingers and called to check.

"This is Duncan Knight. I'm calling regarding the dog I found... the two weeks are up today and I'm hoping I can keep him." I hoped she couldn't hear my voice crack.

"He's all yours, Sir. If you want him."

Through my smile, I asked, "So no one claimed him? I can't believe it. He is the best dog!"

"Well, not exactly. There was a guy who came in holding a flier, claiming the dog was his. But, the thing is, he had no proof at all. He didn't even have a proper address. So we wouldn't consider allowing him to adopt a pet from us, regardless."

I thanked her and hung up. Next, I canceled the ad. I drove around the village and pulled down all the flyers. As far as I was concerned, he was mine. I had already named him Hank. I attached a tag with his name and my address and phone number to his red leather collar. At home, it was as if he was familiar with everything. I never had to train him. He knew the commands of "sit," "stay" and "down" and when he needed to go out to potty, he sat by the door and waited patiently to be let out. At first, we thought he might bolt when we let him out, but he showed no interest in leaving us. He did his business and came right back in. He instantly loved my parents, choosing my dad to sit next to and press his weight against. Eventually, he was allowed on the sofa. I was even more thankful not to have to give him up when I caught my dad cooing, "Who's a good boy? That's right. You're the best boy. Hank is the best boy," while petting him and flipping him bits of cheese.

I had a dog growing up. We said goodbye when I was 16. He was a rusty-colored, mid-sized mutt named Rusty, with no manners and not too bright, but loyal and loving and sweet to all humans and animal-kind. He was 16 too, and after his death, we never got another. It was just too hard. When Hank came home, the three of us wondered how we had ever lived without him and why we had waited so long to get another dog. According to my mom, he chose me, chose us, for his family. That seemed right. This was the sign I needed that something so wonderful could appear from such a negative place. It felt like forgiveness was being granted. I could relax a little.

1999

M Y USUAL ANSWER WOULD have been a solid no. One
of the other agents was hosting a party and the entire
office was attending and it would have looked really obvious
if I didn't.

"You'll be there. Right Knight? It'll be a blast, promise."
This was Ramon, whose office was the nearest mine and
whose bright idea it was to throw this shindig. Ramon is one
of those guys in his 40s who strives to be relevant and cool.
I like him well enough, but I think he tries a little too hard
to impress people.

"Absolutely, I wouldn't miss it for anything," I found
myself responding. There was a theme. 80s. I was not willing
to fashion my hair into a mullet, and ever since I started
earning my own money, I donate all my clothes to charity
once a year. Therefore, I had nothing suitable to wear to this
party that I didn't want to go to in the first place. My dad was
glad to let me comb through his closet, but there wasn't anything workable. His wardrobe never changed much. Mom
suggested a thrift store. Of course. I knew on Main Street

downtown there were several them graced with names like *Abused Children's Thrift Store*, of which I always speculated about whose idea that was and how all the other stakeholders just went with it. Anyway, downtown I went to look for proper 80s attire.

I parked in the structure on the third story. I prefer the third story. There's an open stairwell where I can see the ocean as I climb down the stairs, so I always choose to park up there even if spaces are available closer to the first floor. Someone had spilled a large sticky drink right outside my driver's door, and I considered moving the car. I stepped over it muttering under my breath that people are pigs sometimes. I counted the stairs as I descended, an unbreakable habit since childhood. There were 33. It was a gloomy day with clouds overshadowing the sun. A couple of homeless people sat under awnings with tired cardboard signs. A man tried to grab my attention.

"Hey, can you spare something?"

I kept my head down, not engaging, and noticed a syringe on the ground near the man. Pushing down feelings of anger and disgust, I proceeded to the thrift store while planning to chuck some spare change to him on the way back to my car.

I'm not comfortable in thrift stores and don't frequent them. I usually just drop my donations at the backdoor and collect my receipt to write it off on my taxes. Thrift stores always have a funky smell, and this one was no exception. A sign directed customers to "Leave all bags and backpacks up front" another stated, "Smile, your on camera" obviously written by someone who cared little for correct grammar, and a third proclaimed, "All shoplifters will be persecuted." That one made me chuckle as I wondered what type of persecution a shoplifter could expect. The pathway carpet was worn so thin I could see the plywood underneath. I scanned the racks for something fluorescent, maybe some baggy pants and a wide belt, but I settled on a pantsuit of steel gray. The sport coat had wide shoulders accented by shoulder pads, and the pants were pleated and cuffed at the bottom. I thought they were ladies' pants, but I didn't care. I tried not to think about who had worn them before. I added a button-down shirt in a mint shade, which I planned to leave open at the neck. I'd go back to Dad's closet and get some white tube socks and a pair of his solid white sneakers. To complete the look, I found some aviator sunglasses in the case up front and a red plastic watch, reminiscent of the one I'd worn proudly throughout junior high. It was a God-awful look. It was perfect. I was proud of myself for being a good sport and began to think I might actually have a good time at this party.

There were three people in line, so I took another lap around the store rather than stand there. You always hear of people finding treasures worth a fortune that someone unknowingly donated to charity. It couldn't hurt to look. I walked past a circular clothes rack of jackets and there it was. A bright yellow raincoat. My head spun, and I had to sit for a minute to catch my breath. I plopped onto a floral armchair on sale for $25. My pulse raced and my heart threatened to burst from my chest. I began to sweat profusely and swiped my arm across my forehead.

Everyone looked at me and knew I was a murderer. The night came rushing back and with it the certainty that I'd injured or killed someone. But, I reasoned how absurd this was. There had to be a million jackets like this. Finding one in a secondhand store meant nothing. I was just panicking. I grabbed the jacket by the shoulder and pulled it off the rack.

Tell me your story, I thought. It was smudged and appeared well-worn. It was a unisex-size ML. I held it up to scrutinize it. I closed my eyes for a moment and saw the flash of yellow from that night. My body felt the jolt all over again as my mind replayed a version of the experience. With shaky hands, I unzipped the jacket and noticed it was hip-length and had about a four-inch hem. There was a piece missing from the inside where the fabric was doubled over and sewn, a piece of the yellow rubberized fabric. I added the jacket to my stack and stood in the check-out line, holding myself together the best I could.

"Your total is $43.30. Will you be needing a bag, Sir?"

"No, no bag, thanks."

I handed the cashier two twenties and a five and mumbled to keep the change as a donation. As an afterthought, I asked her if there was any way to know where the jacket came from or possibly when it was donated.

"Oh, I can sorta tell you when," she said. "It's been marked down twice, so it's been in the shop for a year or more. As for where it came from, it could be anywhere, no way to know. Most donations are from local folks, though." I thanked her and left.

As I passed the homeless guy, I tossed him a five, keeping my eyes focused ahead, and continued to the parking structure.

"Hey, hey you." He was calling out to me. I turned to look. He was waving the five-dollar bill.

"Thanks. Don't be too hard on yourself. We've all sinned. I get it."

"What the hell does that mean?" I shouted back, knowing I should not engage with a response.

"I know what you did." He pointed at me, or was he

pointing at the jacket? Or was I losing it?

I climbed the stairs of the parking structure, popped the trunk of my car, and tossed in the suit, glasses, and watch. I held the yellow jacket and got into the front seat. Two cars were waiting for my spot and I waved them off, not ready to drive away yet. I needed a minute. I knew I was being irrational. The jacket, and then the crazy guy calling me out. *Did anyone hear that? I should confess, but to whom, to what, I hadn't actually done anything, had I?* When I finally calmed my nerves enough to drive, I headed straight for the beach. I parked in the dirt lot and walked out toward the surf holding the jacket. Though no one was around, I felt exposed, and judged.

The sound of the waves soothed me as always. I calmed down. There was a garbage can by the boardwalk and I considered stuffing in the jacket, but I knew I needed to take it home.

When I compared the jacket with the piece of fabric I'd saved, the pieces seemed to match. Could I assume the person lived? So maybe I was not a murderer. I felt a little comfort. I wasn't able to fit the jacket in the drawer with the other "evidence". It was too large. Instead, I put it on a hanger, pushed aside my other clothes, and hung it in the back of my closet.

2000

M Y COMPUTER, AND EVERYONE else's, didn't crash. The world did not end. I kinda figured it out when, on the other side of the planet, people rang in the new year with the usual fanfare, and nothing changed. The idea that all hell was going to break loose when the clocks and calendars changed over from 99 to 00 was an interesting one which profited the panic merchants who sold people software to fix the problem as well as fueled the imaginations of the loony tunes and conspiracy theorists. I almost bit, but figured I'd take a chance and even if everything crashed, my two-year supply of food stashed in one third of the three-car garage, plus the water from the pool and my dad's gun, should anyone get crazy, would allow me to survive the catastrophe.

I've sunk into myself. I rarely see friends and wonder if there is even a person I could call a close friend anymore. I spend my time at work, at home, playing with Hank, hiking, swimming in the ocean or the pool, and reading. I prefer solitude to company, or at least that's what I tell myself. Socially, other than work-related activities, I am out of practice.

Hudson was the last of my childhood chums to marry. It was important to his fiance that they start their official life together in the year 2000. Celeste is from a large family, but she and Hudson decided a destination wedding would suit them best. Whatever relatives could come, great, but it was all about the bride and groom and close friends of which I am graciously still considered, even after the comic store debacle. Small was better, intimate. Apparently, there have been many babies born and weddings celebrated this year. People feel the year will be lucky. I planned to attend the wedding and leave as soon as I could without seeming rude.

The occasion required me to fly to Cabo San Lucas and stay at a resort for an entire week. I booked my room for five days, knowing that would be plenty for me. This type of activity is not recommended for my anxiety. I'm on meds now. My doctor thought it was best, so did the psychiatrist whom I saw exactly once. Just a Xanax, low dose, as needed, when I feel the panic coming on strong, to control the feeling of my having a heart attack, and to make being in the company of others more tolerable.

For one of the bachelor party festivities, we went deep-sea fishing. Some of the guys got terribly seasick, not me. The entire crew of the boat was wearing yellow slickers, so I had to remain calm. I swear, before the incident, I noticed no one ever wearing that type of raincoat, except the crossing guard, and why now do they seem to be all over the place, taunting me? I can tell myself it's just frequency illusion, a cognitive bias that all humans experience, like when you buy a new car and suddenly everyone is driving the same one everywhere you look, but even this rational self-talk doesn't calm my nerves.

On another day, we rented jet skis. I enjoyed it. We stayed close to shore, but for a minute I felt a strong temptation to point mine out to sea and keep going. I didn't, but having the power to do it if I wanted, felt freeing. I'm considering purchasing a jet ski as a result. Pretty sure I can get Hank to ride along. I can afford it. I don't spend much and have had good sales this year, and there's room in the garage.

It was obvious when I arrived in Cabo that my friends had planned to set me up with the one single female from the bride's side, Hanna. She was nice enough, pretty enough, but no.

Hopefully, I clarified that I'm not interested without being considered rude. It's a delicate balance. I don't want a relationship. Don't need one. Too complicated. I'm not ready. At 27, shouldn't I be, though? Maintaining friends is something I will try to put more effort into. I should initiate activities. I can hold my own in a conversation, but I'm not comfortable with small talk and I fit in okay, but nothing deep, nothing serious. Have I lost that gear? I find that so often when other people are talking, I simply tune out. Then, when I'm spoken to directly, I try to figure out what the conversation is about so I can respond. I've always been like this, I think.

Could be the ADD. It's not that I don't like people. If there is a purpose and an activity, I'm good and comfortable just to be.

I don't know how to reminisce, either. Truth is, I recall little of my school years. They weren't terrible. I obviously had friends and did stuff, but if you press me, I'm short on the details. And of my early life, my memories are even sketchier. As a kid, I fixated on one idea or activity and whatever that was, it would occupy all my thoughts, time, and effort. Take Tae Kwon Do, it was my singular focus for two years. Then

I lost interest, and that was it. I never looked back. The belts I earned are still curled up in a shoebox saved lovingly by Mom. I was up to green belt level when I quit.

On the fourth night in Cabo, we were gathered in Celeste's suite, which she was sharing with her bridal party members. The wedding was scheduled for the following afternoon. I planned to spend that night and leave early the next morning, skipping the celebration breakfast and final beach day. Wet swimsuits hanging over chairs, empty wine coolers strewn about, and a heavy scent of coconut sunscreen filled the place. On the dining table she had spread out old photos and was constructing a collage with the help of the other ladies. This would be displayed at the reception and the guests would all sign their names around it as a memento of the big day. I scanned the table. There were bound to be photos of me from back in the day. Hudson and I have practically known each other from birth. Our moms met at some program for new mothers run by the hospital nursing staff. We'd been together in a playgroup, then preschool, and all the way through high school. We were fixtures in each other's lives growing up. Hudson's parents are older like mine and we are both only children, so the sort of forced friendship was inevitable. Not to say that I don't like him, I do, as much as I can like anyone.

As I inspected the photos, I noticed myself in several. And I saw another boy in two of the group shots. I had forgotten about him. He was taller than the rest of us, huskier too, and was wearing the same army-style pants in the three photos I saw him in.

"What grade were we in here?" I asked Hudson, pointing at one photo.

"Looks like maybe third or fourth. I think that was a Boy

38

Scout trip, remember?"

"Oh yeah. Who is this kid?"

"Are you kidding? How do you not remember? That's Barty, Barton Miller. That kid was a psycho! Remember how he jumped in that swampy pond and my dad had to fish him out?"

I vaguely remembered and asked, "What happened to him? Didn't he leave our school, or get expelled or something?"

"I don't know if he actually got expelled, but he left during 6th grade. I think his family life was pretty jacked up. That kid was always in trouble. He broke a toilet at school once and blamed me for it. He taught us all the bad words, and we were the ones to end up in trouble, and he instructed us all on the facts of life too, with a lot of misinformation, I might add." Hudson laughed at this. It was coming back to me now.

"Now I remember," I said a little too loudly.

"He tossed buckets of dirt and rocks in our pool when he was over once. And threw a baseball through the window of the guest house. My parents were really pissed, but I guess they felt sorry for him. I didn't like him. He weirded me out. I didn't want him to come over, but my mom insisted. I think she felt sorry for him. You're right, his family life was a mess. He bragged that his dad was in jail and I think his mom was a drug addict or alcoholic. Maybe he got taken away from them," I speculated, and looked up to notice I apparently had the full attention of everyone in the room.

"What?" I asked, to no one in particular.

"Nothing," Celeste said. "It's just that I've never heard you talk so much. You've always been so quiet."

"Oh, sorry. I guess I have a lot on my mind. I'm closing a couple of deals, so I'm distracted."

Then she said, "I remember Barty Miller from high school. He went to Mesa. And you're right, he really was a weirdo, super strange. In English, I sat at his desk once. You'd have thought he owned it or something. He got right in my face and told me to get out. When he grabbed my arm, I moved. I think he would've tossed me to the floor otherwise. He was a loose cannon. No one messed with him. Everyone knew his dad was in jail and there were plenty of rumors about what he did to get there. Then in junior year, his mom committed suicide. Jumped off a cliff, I think. He disappeared after that. Dropped out. Some girls were disappointed. They thought he was dangerous, and they liked that sort of thing. Word was he ended up in jail for stealing. A few years ago, a friend of mine mentioned she thought she saw him in town, begging. I guess he was homeless. Pretty sad." Celeste took a sip of her wine cooler and tossed her hair over her shoulder. She didn't seem all that sad about Barty's fate.

"He was always stealing from the other kids at school," Hudson added.

"Yeah, he used to take food from the pantry at my house and stuff it in his backpack. When I told him to put it back, he punched me. That's how he was. Volatile," I said.

The thought of a childhood acquaintance, now being homeless, did not sit well with me at all, even if it was someone I never liked.

"Well, we all know the homeless aren't tolerated in the village, too unseemly. I heard the cops pick them up and drop them off a few miles away," Hanna chimed in, "at least that's what my brother-in-law told me. He's a police officer."

This is true. It is relatively rare to see a homeless person in the village proper. It simply won't do. But just because we don't see them, doesn't mean they aren't there. I'm guilty of calling the police when I noticed a man sleeping in the bushes behind Village Real Estate. I was expecting clients from the valley and that was not the first impression I hoped to make. Police arrived promptly, removed the fellow, and tossed his belongings in the dumpster. I never asked where they took him. I honestly didn't care. I was just thankful it all went down before my clients arrived or it might've cost me a sale.

The wedding of Hudson and Celeste was small, about 50 people, and took place on a grassy area, cliffside, overlooking the ocean. They had written their own vows, and since it wasn't a church wedding, the whole ceremony took less than 30 minutes. I focused on the vows. "I promise to always be there for you, keep you safe, take care of you." *Would I be able to say this to another person someday?* At the reception, I signed my name on the finished picture collage and found myself fixating again on memories from my youth. In three years, I would be 30. Would my life be any different from the way it was now? I ate my chicken dinner, and joined the group for the Macarena and the YMCA dances, and did tequila shots with the boys. I was a proper wedding guest.

The cake was cut and eaten and one last request was made of the guests. Celeste's sister took the microphone and said, "Please write your best wishes or advice for the new couple on one of these note cards, and put it in this vase. We want the couple to read them if they are having a tough time. We want them to know they will always have all of our love and support in their new life together." *Pretty sappy*, I thought, but what the heck. I grabbed a note card and wrote, "Keep no secrets." I figured that was some sage wisdom.

My flight was early the next morning, so I took the airport shuttle van from the resort before anyone else from the wedding was even awake. Goodbye, Cabo. I chose a window seat, put on my headphones, and pretended to sleep so the passenger next to me, an older lady, would not attempt conversation. After two hours, I got up to use the restroom, and she was engrossed in a book and seemed equally uninterested in chatting. I arrived at the airport; retrieved my car from the valet and drove home. I still had a good portion of the day left but chose not to go into the office. I would check my email from home and just rest and re-group for the remainder of the day.

As soon as I pulled into the driveway, I was greeted by Hank, who was positively beside himself with joy to see me. There is nothing like being greeted by your dog after being away for a few days to make you feel like a celebrity. He was wiggling, slobbering, and jumping all over me. I set down my suitcase and sat in the driveway laughing while being playfully attacked with kisses and licks. Dad walked over.

"That's quite a welcome. Glad you're back, Son. We miss you when you're not around." He bent down and gave me a pat on the back.

"What are you doing at home, Dad? I thought you'd be in the office."

"Nah, not going in today. Mom's got lunch ready. Come eat with us."

"Sounds great. Let me put my stuff down and I'll be right in."

I put my things in the pool house, kicked off my shoes, changed into shorts, and wondered if everything was okay with my parents. Sure, my dad could choose when to go into the office, but why today? I met my parents in the kitchen where my mom was setting tuna salad sandwiches on a tray to take outside. She greeted me with a warm hug. I had to know and blurted out, "Are you guys okay? Is everything okay?"

A look passed between them and then Mom said, "Yes, yes, we're fine. We had a little scare though. Your father had a biopsy of a polyp. The doctor removed it during the procedure he had. You remember, the colonoscopy."

"Is it cancer?"

"No, it's benign."

"I'm fine, Dunc. It's common for an old guy like me. Just goes with the territory."

"You should have told me."

"We don't like to worry you. We wanted you to enjoy the wedding."

"Well, from now on, can you please keep me in the loop? If something's wrong, I need to know. Please don't try to spare me. I'm not a little kid. I'm almost 30."

"You'll always be a little kid to us. Besides, 27 is not almost 30."

We took the trays to the outside table and sat down for lunch. I told my parents all about the wedding and showed them the few pictures I'd snapped on my digital camera. Then I asked them about Barty Miller. They recalled him well.

"That poor boy. He really had it rough. Remember your teacher in second grade? She was a friend of mine. She shared with me how difficult Barton's family life was and asked me to encourage a friendship between you boys."

"Why did you let him keep coming home with me even after he broke the window and threw dirt in our pool?" I asked.

"We were trying to teach you to be empathetic, that not everyone has it as easy as you," Dad said.

43

"Oh."

I took a bite of my sandwich and let that sink in. I felt guilty then. Barty was constantly asking to come over and I would repeatedly make excuses or say I was going to Hudson's house. I was not nice or empathetic, but I was just a kid. The visits eventually became less frequent, but he got meaner toward me and wanted to do things that would get us in trouble. I decided it was best not to elaborate too much and doubted my parents would see it the same way I did.

"So, what made you think of him after all this time? Was he at the wedding?" Mom asked hopefully. I could tell she was curious.

"No, Hudson and Celeste had pictures of him and it struck a memory, that's all. One girl in the bridal party went to high school with him. Truthfully, I hadn't thought of him in years, but now I wonder where he is and what he's up to. If he's okay. Another girl in the bridal party heard he was homeless a few years ago."

"Oh Duncan, that's really sad if it's true."

"Yes, it is," I agreed.

"Well, I don't suppose there is anything we can do."

"No, I don't suppose there is."

Even so, I felt plagued by the thought of someone I knew being homeless. I flashed back to the man who yelled at me outside the thrift store last year and how it shook me so deeply. I avoid the homeless. I avert my eyes, not wanting to think of them as actual people with feelings. I'm embarrassed. For me? For them? I don't know. Aren't they all just hopeless drug addicts?

Can't they help themselves if they care to? Why is it my responsibility? I know Mom feels differently. She was instrumental in starting a chapter of Helping Hands at their,

I mean our, church. They now have enough volunteers and donations to make and serve lunches five days a week out of the parish kitchen. The lunches are available for anyone who wants them. No questions. No need to verify who you are. There are picnic benches and portable hand washing stations set up in addition to the restrooms. They are trying to raise funds for portable laundry stations and showers to be brought in twice a month as well. Mom has spoken about it often at dinner. I know she'd love it if I dropped by, but I haven't. I should. Maybe I'll send a donation.

2001

I SHOW AND SELL homes with obscene price tags. My listings and sales seem oddly clustered around the area of the incident. Almost every property is on Ocean View Road and has a view from one or more balconies or the back of the property, not just of the ocean, but of the very spot I had imagined I'd hit something driving home that night six years ago. Originally, I didn't think I could identify the exact place where it happened, but as time went on, I realized I was drawn inexplicably to a particular place with a large twisty tree and I have come to think of it as *the place*. Still living in my parents' pool house, still no plans to leave. I could easily afford a nice place of my own, but I'm comfortable with the way things are. I don't care what anyone thinks. And they enjoy having me. I'm their only child, so there's no competition for their affection and no one to compare me to. They need me. And after Dad's medical scare, there is no way I'm moving out.

Most of the time, I focus on my job or other responsibilities and just live my life the best I can. A few months ago

I showed a house on Ocean View to a couple who were looking in the two to four million dollar range. This didn't impress me, as it is always the case with my clients, and Ocean View properties are all in this range or higher, if you can even find one for sale. As with many of my clients, we are still in touch. I like to send holiday cards and greetings to keep me on my clients' radar. Okay, so my mom actually does this. And it was her idea. Brilliant, though. People love it, I think.

So about the couple, the man is older than his wife. He looks to be in his mid-sixties and she could pass for thirties, though you never know how big a role surgical intervention has played. Truthfully, I liked them from the start. Still do. He's a barrel chested, short guy, with bowed legs and a distinctive limp. He always wears golf shorts and a polo shirt, white socks pulled up and sneakers that look like square white bricks. A gold cross hangs on a thick chain from his neck. Large glasses make his eyes look wide open, and he still has an impressive amount of hair on his head, dyed jet black with a bit of silver at the roots. She's a stereotypical trophy wife. Long dark chestnut hair teased up in the front, bright ocean blue eyes and brilliant white teeth, probably veneers, tanned and toned, like a thousand other women who roam the village walking their puffy little dogs between salon visits, personal training sessions, charity and church events, and coffee chats with friends. Herb and Margie are their names.

I showed them a property higher than their price range knowing she'd love it and he, wanting to keep the peace and keep her happy, would oblige. Sure enough. I first showed the only other two properties available in their target area. Both homes were dated and needed work. The third property was the show-stopper. Italian marble floors through-out, overblown chandeliers, gaudy gold accents everywhere. There was a double spiral staircase and an elevator. Six bedrooms all with en suite baths, each unique and taste specific and a separate maid or nanny living space. It was so over-the-top you couldn't help but be impressed even if it wasn't your taste. It was a space for entertaining, opulent, and pretentious. Outside was the full outdoor kitchen with professional appliances and an infinity pool overlooking the edge of the mountain with an ocean view. The guest house was much nicer than the one I live in at my parents' house. Margie smiled at Herb, and it was over. They had me write a full asking price offer that evening, not wanting anyone else to swoop in and take their dream house. I didn't even need to go into my spiel about how many others were considering purchasing the place, of course, there were none.

She just needed to smile the smile that didn't reach her eyes or crinkle her forehead, it was all the Botox would allow, and he was butter.

As I said, I like this couple. Herb is such a gregarious man, friendly and honest to a fault.

He made his millions and wants to enjoy it. We golfed together. He added my name to his membership and invited me to go have lunch anytime and just put it on his tab. We hung out more frequently, golfing usually once a week. I was pretty proud of myself for cultivating a friendship. Herb seemed to genuinely enjoy my company. Often Margie would join us for lunch.

"After all, I can't ever thank the guy who sold us our dream house enough, can I? And I'm glad you're willing to golf with an old lame-leg dude like me."

"How did you injure it Herb, if you don't mind my asking?" I was curious.

"The thing of it is," Herb always begins a story this way, "I used to drink too much. Not just a little too much. A lot too much. Margie considered leaving me because of it."

"Oh Herb, you know that's not true, I'd never leave you my love," and she leaned over to plant a kiss on his cheek, leaving behind a smudge of pink lipstick.

"Not the point. You should have. I was awful. An ass. I'd have deserved it. So, back to my bum leg. Hell, at one point it was my entire right side. I was paralyzed, you know? It's nothing but a miracle I can walk. Months of therapy it took. Months of Miguel yelling at me to get off my butt, try harder. 'You can do it buddy, I believe in you.' Then one fine day, I literally got off my ass and walked again. It was a God damned miracle Knight. A miracle." With this declaration, he slapped me on the back and he looked me dead in the eyes.

"So you fell down when you were drunk one night and broke your hip or something?" I asked.

"No, I didn't fall and break my hip. Some jackass mowed me down on the road and nearly killed me!"

"Wait, what!?" There was no way to maintain my composure, but I tried to as the panic rose within me.

"Yeah, a hit and run. Back in June of '95. I never found out who it was. Never really tried either. It was just the wake up call I needed, if I'm honest. I was at a party and I'd had way too much, got into a bit of a spat with an old friend, then took off on a walk to cool down in the middle of the night. Stupid of me."

He ran his fingers through his hair and his eyes looked up at the ceiling, then deep into mine.

"The jerk-off probably saved my life." His wife chimes in.

"I wanted to report it. I thought the person should pay for what they did, but Herb was insistent. I'm just glad he's okay. That's all that matters now."

I left. I went home and floated in the pool on my oversized raft for an hour and fell asleep. I woke up with my thoughts racing. Should I tell Herb that I, the golden boy, almost killed him? Why should I? I was effectively off the hook for good. It was official. And I, in all actuality, had saved this guy, saved his marriage and his health, and in the end it cost him six months of therapy and a prominent limp some would call charming for an old guy. I'm a savior. Not a killer. I did a good deed. So why don't I feel good?

The next time I saw Herb at the golf course, after a round and a couple of beers in the clubhouse, I decided to come clean.

"Herb, about your limp," I began, already feeling the weight lifting as I prepared my confession, "I've been thinking about it, and man, I feel just awful."

"Not sure why you'd feel awful, Knight. That's the least of the shit that happened to me in Tennessee. I could tell you more stories, but I don't want you to think less of me!" He was laughing.

"Tennessee?"

2002

I DECIDED TO GET trained along with Dad for disaster preparedness.

"Duncan, are you interested in this? We could do it together," he pointed to an advertisement in the Village Reporter, *Volunteers Needed: Disaster Preparedness Training.*

"No promises, Dad. You know how busy I am, but I'll go to the meeting with you and see what's required."

The meeting place was the cramped office of the water district. Nine people showed up.

Honestly, more than I expected. It was an eight-week commitment, possibly more, strictly volunteer. Meetings would be on Saturdays from 10-1pm. Bring your own lunch and drinks. The man in charge was all business and looked like he was a military guy. His tone was serious as he explained, "If we can't count on your full support for the duration of the eight weeks, it's best you leave now."

He needed a clue on how to sell, that's for certain. When we stepped outside for an "eight-minute break," I said, "Dad, this guy's intense, a total drill sergeant. Does he not realize this is voluntary and we don't have to be here? He's going to lose his audience and all his volunteers. I'm not sure about this commitment."

"True. But let's have fun with it. We don't get to hang out together much; and we should contribute to our community. We can think of it like we're back in the Boy Scouts. Just let 'Mr. In Charge' do his thing. Don't let it get to you." Dad understands how I don't care for authority figures. Never have.

"Sure, I can do that. It'll be good for me to volunteer." I knew this was true, but I always lacked the motivation to follow through, and here was my opportunity.

So we committed to the next eight Saturdays, and I have to say, Dad was right. I gained valuable information and knowledge. We created a map of where to evacuate in case of an emergency. Each street in the Upper and Lower Village has a specific route and an alternate route. This will prevent backups and let evacuations flow smoothly if ever an evacuation is called for. A letter was drafted and sent to the residents of the Upper and Lower Village of Oceanview. Households were encouraged to devise and submit their own individual plans, make a get-away first aid kit and emergency supply bag, and follow the suggestions put forth regarding what to do if our area experienced a prolonged power outage or water shut-off. Few owners in the Upper Village were without generators, including us. If you could afford it, why be inconvenienced by an outage? The village, both upper and lower, is far enough from the beach that we don't have to consider the threat of either a tsunami or storm surge. If either were to happen, our community center would serve as a temporary shelter for people living in the lower elevations closer to the coast. Mr. In-Charge requested that we sign up to volunteer at the shelter if needed. I did not add my name to that list.

Wildfire is possible, I suppose, but there hasn't been one in forever, and residents have to keep the bushes cleared from their properties, so I think we're okay there. The real reason for this project is the mayor of our little town wants bragging rights that every homeowner is prepared for a disaster. If we follow the recommendations, he will be able to put the designation on the town website and it can be a feather in his cap when he tries to run for a more prestigious office and move up the local political ladder. Of course, he's been conspicuously absent from the eight-week commitment.

I signed up to keep track of which residents had submitted their emergency plans and information. Rather than do it myself, I enlisted Mom to write and send out an email reminder and a second letter by regular mail to each house that didn't initially respond. I know the area well because of my profession, but there are a few properties I was interested in checking out more closely, and any chance to make a new connection might lead to a new client and a large sale and commission. There is not a single property worth under a million in the Upper Village. California coastal properties are always sought after.

"I can go door to door to the homes that haven't submitted their emergency plans," I offered.

"Perfect," said Mr. In-Charge who we learned had the real name of Gordon Foxworth. We waited a few days for the holdouts to turn in their plans. It wasn't required, of course, but I too wanted the designation on our Ocean View website, and we needed 95% compliance of homeowners to get it. I had something to gain from this. I think buyers new to the area will be impressed knowing we have a "Comprehensive Disaster Plan" especially one that I can say I was instrumental in putting together.

Dad sat in the passenger seat and held the list. He directed me to the first house. We didn't know the people. They were friendly and happily complied with the request to complete their emergency plans and resident information.

"Honestly, though, we're relocating to Georgia in six months," the wife said, "so I suppose the new owners will need to make their own plan."

"Yes. We're creating a database that will be updated as residents move in and out. I'm also thinking about a directory, so neighbors can get to know each other, if they choose to opt-in. It can be tricky when all our houses are so far apart and so private. Do you have an agent yet, for when you're ready to sell?"

"We used Ramon from Village Realty when we bought it two years ago."

"Yes. He's a colleague of mine, a great guy. He rarely focuses on this area though, whereas the Upper Village is my specialty. I'll leave you my card. And thanks again for your cooperation."

Dad and I made our way to three more houses where we were successful in signing up the occupants, as well as leaving my business cards. I felt productive. Our last stop was at the top of the mountain. There were only a few houses here. Huge palatial estates with terraced yards and private driveways. The property we were seeking was not one of these. It was one of the last remaining that had not been upgraded or modernized in any way. The circular driveway desperately needed repaving. My Lexus seemed to hit every pothole, and I was concerned about the alignment, not to mention the dirt I was kicking up because I'd taken the car in for a full detail two days earlier. I take it twice a month or more if it gets dusty. The black finish seems to really show the dirt, and I like it shiny. It's one of the few luxuries I enjoy. Well, my car and my clothes. I need to look the part of a successful real estate professional. It's working.

"Should we even bother with this house? It looks abandoned," Dad remarked.

"I think this is the front side of the old property we used to sneak into as kids to drink beers. I probably shouldn't give away that secret, Dad, but I'm old enough now so I won't get busted," I laughed.

"Hilarious, Duncan. You should know that your mother and I and most of the parents were well aware of the abandoned party shed. We figured it was harmless fun. I'm glad I didn't know about the underage drinking, though."

"Like you said, Dad. Harmless fun. Ages ago."

We exited the car and approached the home. It was in a serious state of disrepair. All the trees were overgrown, and some were dead dried skeletons that would make perfect tinder.

Broken-off branches were left where they fell. The house was in obvious violation of the brush-clearing ordinance. The window frames were disintegrating, and the glass was opaque. I could see termite droppings in piles on the deck under the eaves. The ancient, gray, peeling paint gave the entire structure the appearance of being enveloped in a moldy coating. Roof shingles were missing in large patches, which would, of course, result in water damage inside. I doubted this dump was salvageable. If it ever sold, it would require a tear-down and complete rebuild.

Still, this piece of land was worth millions, and if the landscaping was done properly, the view would be incredible.

I thought about the possibilities.

"Anybody home?" I shouted as I knocked on the front door. No response, but there was an older model car in the driveway with flat tires. I knocked again. No answer.

"I don't think they're home. Who are we looking for Dad?"

"Mr. Kerigan," Dad answered.

"Hey, let's take a peek around the back. Maybe he's outside and can't hear us."

We walked around the side of the house and through an open gate, also in desperate need of repair. A rusty *No Trespassing* sign was hanging by one corner. The property was graded here, with a large arena, the fencing rotten and falling down. It was a horse property at one time. There were a couple of smaller pens and, toward the back, I could see the old shed. We had accessed it as kids from the back way on a short-cut off the trail.

"Did you see that, Dad?" I think someone is down at the shed.

"Who's there?" I called out, cupping my hands around my mouth to project my voice. A scruffy man in a flannel shirt and dirty jeans appeared, saw us, then turned and ran down the hillside, disappearing from sight.

"We should probably leave. Technically, we're trespassing, even if it is for a good reason," Dad said, and I remembered the old man who used to threaten us as kids saying he had a gun.

We'd just laughed and run away. Suddenly, this seemed like a bad idea and it didn't feel safe. What was I thinking, putting my dad in danger? "Yes, time to leave," I agreed.

We trekked back to my car just as an older model Ford truck pulled into the driveway.

The driver, an old man with shoulder-length white hair wearing a baseball cap, rolled down his window and yelled at us, "Who are you? What do you want?"

"Hi there, are you Mr. Kerigan?"

"Who wants to know? You're trespassing! Get off my property before I get my shotgun." He leaned over the seat and reached into the back. I didn't want to stick around at that point and felt the chances of this character complying with our request were slim, but I asked anyway.

"We're helping folks put together emergency plans. We'd like to assist you if you're interested."

"I'm not interested! And you shouldn't be here!"

"Sure, we were just leaving. Sorry to bother you," I spoke while we jumped into my car and I started the engine.

"We'll just have him be part of the 5% who don't participate," Dad said as we pulled away.

"Agreed. I think that's the same old guy from years ago. Funny how some people look old your whole life," I mused.

And Dad replied, "That's enough excitement for today. Let's go to the Village Tavern and have a beer. We've earned it, unless you've got work to do."

"No, I think a beer would be perfect."

2003

R AMON IS NOW THE Head Realtor in our office at Village
Realty. The title does not signify much as we are all our
own independent agents, but I know for a fact, it means a lot
to him. He likes the title and enjoys his self-appointed role as
Official Team Builder. He calls meetings where we discuss
the "company image" including our office design, logo, and
yearly slogan. Currently, the slogan is, "It's more than just
your home. It's your life." I think it's lame. What does that
even mean?

I was not surprised when Ramon took his ideas for
team-building to the next level.

"Ok, folks. Listen up. I'd like us to build our bond as
co-workers and friends. We're like a family here at Village
Realty, and I've budgeted a fun activity that we all can enjoy."
I was not aware a budget existed for this type of thing,
but ok. He continued, "I've reserved the entire facility at
Mountain Sports for an afternoon of zip lining." He paused
for effect. "Put it on your calendars, June 10th, 4-7 pm.
Just deal with any important business by 3 that day, and

leave your afternoon and evening available. We can arrange carpools, and it's only 45 minutes away. Dinner afterward."

All of my office mates were enthusiastic, even Gus Maxwell who said he was too old for zip lining, but would gladly film the rest of us. Same with Adriene Short, whom I've never seen dressed in anything but a skirt and heels and who is at least 75. She said she would attend but would not be, "hanging from a rope, shooting down a mountainside."

Zip lining was something I had always wanted to do but hadn't gotten around to and couldn't think of anyone to ask to go with me. I was thrilled with the idea. To make sure I would not forget or schedule anything else for that afternoon, I wrote it in my day planner at work and as soon as I got home, I wrote it in large print on my calendar desk blotter then circled it in fluorescent yellow for emphasis. June 10th. It would be good to have plans and a distraction on a day that I looked forward to with dread each year. I tried not to relive the incident, but on June 10th, it was always difficult not to.

Mom's reaction was similar to Adriene's.

"Honey, that seems dangerous. Couldn't you hurt your back doing that?" I assured her I'd be fine. She had two weeks to calm down about it. I don't like upsetting her. She was already a little worked up about me spending some nights at Herb and Margie's house. They were gone for a month to the south of France and asked me to monitor the place, but to also feel free to stay there as much as I liked. Just before leaving, they had heard about some properties in the Upper Village being broken into. Each property was isolated and, in every case, the owners had left for an extended period of time. Shortly after purchasing their mini-mansion, Herb had a top-of-the-line security system installed, but Margie said she'd just be more comfortable with someone staying there, if I wouldn't mind.

"Please make yourself at home. Use the gym, the pool, the sauna. And you know we've got an impressive collection of movies in the theater."

"I'd be happy to look in on the house for you and spend some nights there, no problem," I said. I didn't mind at all. Plus, Hank was welcome too, so it would be like a brief vacation for me, never mind that is only about a mile from where I live.

I planned on spending a couple nights a week at Herb's and Margie's and would let my parents know in advance so they would not expect me home and worry. So, one afternoon, I stopped by after work. I hadn't checked their house for a few days, and I didn't have my bag to spend the night, but after helping myself to a beer, then another and another, and soaking in the hot tub, I retired to the theater room, wearing only my boxers and wrapped in a plush robe, to put in a movie and sober up. I called home and said I'd be late.

"Hey Dad, let Mom know I'm working late over at Herb and Margie's place. Don't save me dinner. I'm getting a pizza." I did not need to mention the multiple beers I'd consumed.

I chose a silly romantic comedy and settled into one of the leather recliners, ultimately relaxed. I awoke startled and disoriented when I heard pounding on the front door. The movie had finished, and it was completely dark now except for the blue screen. I noticed the digital clock read 10:15. Jumping up and wrapping the robe around me, I ran to the door and threw it wide open without thinking. There stood two security officers. Rubbing the sleep from my eyes, I asked what was going on.

"We got an alert of a disturbance here, Sir. Who are you?"

"I'm house-sitting for the Goldmans. My name is Knight. Duncan Knight. Can I grab my wallet? I'll show you my ID."

The officers followed me in and once I produced my driver's license they explained what happened.

"Mr. Goldman let us know you might be staying here. We received a security alert that an outside door was being tampered with. The Goldman's have 24-hour surveillance trained on all points of entry. We pulled up the footage and saw a man trying the door. He tripped a motion sensor light and took off. We headed right over to check it out."

"Wow. I've grown up here in the Upper Village my entire life and there was never any crime. No one even locked their doors, it being so isolated."

"There still isn't much, just recently, a few break-ins. The police are on it. They think it's the same perpetrator or perpetrators. They seem to know when folks are gone, so they must be local and watching. That's our theory."

The officers searched the grounds. There was no damage to the door and they could not collect fingerprints. The suspect was wearing gloves. Boot prints showed he had walked under the windows and he left a muddy smear on the landing by the door he'd tried. When the security officers left, I stayed the night. Whoever was here had to be long gone. I was exhausted and didn't feel like driving home. But after the disruption, I never got comfortable and once the sun came up and it was light out, I changed back into yesterday's clothes and drove home. Dad's an early riser so I entered the main house hoping coffee would be ready, and it was. Hank lumbered over after doing his morning downward doggie stretches and greeted me with a couple of licks and a wagging tail.

"What time did you finally get in, Dunc? I see you slept in your clothes."

"Oh, I decided..." I started to say but was interrupted by my mom.

"You were up so late. I saw your light on after 1."

"No, Mom, I just came home. I stayed at the Goldmans' after all. I fell asleep and actually got woken by their security guys. I was just going to tell Dad about it. Apparently, someone tried to break in. While I was there."

My mom looked visibly flustered. "No, honey, you were here. I saw you in the pool house last night, late."

"No, I just got home now, just a little while ago. I stayed over there but didn't sleep well. That's why I'm in yesterday's clothes."

I did not want to upset Mom or make her think she was wrong or forgetful. Dad said, "Maybe you're thinking of another night, Linda. Here, let me get you a cup of coffee."

"I suppose you're right. I swear I saw you walking around with the lamp on, though. But, I guess not. Have you been in the pool house yet? Maybe you just left the light on."

To reassure Mom, I replied, "Yes, that's probably it. I must have left the light on yesterday. Sorry about that. I'll be more careful." I grabbed two toaster pastries, a banana, and a large mug of coffee and left, explaining I still needed to shower and was going to the office early. I needed to take care of a property management situation. I did not want to consider that both my parents were getting older. I didn't want to think that Mom might be losing her memory, becoming forgetful, or seeing things that weren't there. They will never get old and will always be here for me. I want to believe.

I turned my key in the door of the pool house and stepped

inside, looking forward to a hot shower. The tall lamp in the corner was on. It's not connected to the light switch, and it's not a lamp I ever use. I certainly would not have left it on yesterday morning when I was last home.

Weird. And then I noticed that smell of damp earth and my skin prickled. Nothing was missing, nothing was disturbed, at least that I could see. I compulsively opened my sock drawer and felt for the piece of rubber fabric and the fortune cookie fortune. Both were there, and I mentally chided myself for being paranoid. Still, I looked in my closet to check for the yellow jacket. It too, was undisturbed. The atmosphere felt strange though, off. That's the only way I can describe it.

Before I knew it, June 10th arrived. All the agents met in the parking lot of Village Realty. Carpools were arranged. I would ride with Ramon. I regretted this choice after I folded myself into the passenger seat of his little Alfa Romeo sports car and began feeling carsick on the way up the mountain. Ramon is perpetually single, but looking for a serious relationship. He regaled me with his dating tales and asked me about my love life.

"There isn't much to tell," I explained. "I don't really know how to ask out women." That was a mistake. Ramon treated me to his version of Dating 101: For the Complete Idiot. I could not wait to get to Mountain Sports to make this topic of conversation end.

When we arrived, we were given a safety briefing and shown how to put on the harness, and helmet, after signing a waiver agreeing not to hold Mountain Sports liable if an injury or worse should occur. An open-air tram took us to the first line. We hiked up to the platform, and it was at that point we noticed it was a sheer drop-off. The cable looked very thin, and I wondered about the integrity of the clips. We were expected to stand on the platform, get into a squat position and then jump, trusting the cable would hold until we reached the other end, where another staff member would undo the clip. A perky girl in her 20s did a quick demonstration explaining before she lept, "You can hang upside down if you want, or make yourself spin." I glanced around, sensing that some of us were rethinking this activity.

"Who's first?" The 20-something male instructor looked at our group expectantly.

Ramon volunteered to go first. He made it across, and one by one, we all mustered the courage to leap. The feeling was incredible, so worth it. Each successive line was longer and steeper than the last.

On the 5th line, the instructors passed out bean bags and encouraged us to try to hit a target. Whoever got closest would win a prize. I was last to go. I held the beanbag and prepared to drop it at precisely the right moment to land on the target. About halfway, I heard a high-pitched whistle coming from my left side. I turned my head to look, and I saw it. A crumpled body slumped over a patch of sharp rocks. The legs were bare and twisted at an unnatural angle. I could only see a little of the head. The upper body was clothed in a yellow windbreaker. Next thing I knew, my legs hit the edge of the platform. I had reached the end of the 5th line and was still clutching my beanbag. I scrambled to the platform and shouted, "Did you guys see that? There's a body down there. A dead body. Oh my God."

"I suppose that's why you didn't toss your beanbag?" Ramon remarked nonchalantly.

I shook and, to my horror, cried. "No, it's a body. Someone is dead. I'm not kidding around."

"Sometimes your eyes can play tricks on you," said the male instructor, "But we'll go check it out when we collect the bean bags. Here, come sit down and have some water. It's boiling today. Heatstroke is no joke. Have you been drinking enough water?" He handed me a cold water bottle from a cooler.

I took some deep breaths and tried to regain my composure. Everyone was avoiding eye contact with me. No one had seen a dead body and my distress was making them uncomfortable. I didn't do the 6th and last zipline. We sat on the bench of the open-air tram to wait for the other people to finish. I was quiet during the BBQ, my stomach in knots. I know what I saw. The instructors called me aside and reported that they had looked all around under the 5th line and there was no dead body. I asked if they could take me with them in the all-terrain golf cart to see for myself, not caring if they thought I was crazy. They did and stopped the cart under line five. I hopped out and looked around.

"Who has access to this area? Is it open to the public?" I asked the kid who was driving the golf cart.

"It's pretty isolated. I mean, it's not gated off or anything, but, Dude, no one comes here. There's no reason to, except for staff, especially under the lines." I found the location where I thought I'd seen something.

"What is this red mark on this boulder?" I asked.

I swear the kid rolled his eyes before responding, "It's paint, okay? Red paint."

And yes, that is what it looked like, an old smudge of red paint. No body, nothing disturbed or out of place. There were footprints all around, but there was a logical explanation for that. Staff was frequently underline five to set up the targets and collect the beanbags afterward. There was undeniably nothing there. Yet, I know what I saw.

Was I having a delusion? The thought was terrifying.

2004

M<small>Y CHURCH ATTENDANCE OVER</small> the years has been sporadic at best. I try to pray every day and ask for forgiveness and I try to be a good person, but the services, well, let's just say, I find I'm often busy or they aren't at a convenient time for me. A good real estate agent should be available for his clients or potential clients on Sundays. When I attend, my mind wanders. The idea of greeting people makes my anxiety flare and the closeness to others is not for me. But being in the building when it's empty and quiet, seeing the altar, feeling God's presence, this I crave, and it calms me.

"Mom, do you know if there are times when St. Mark's is just open for prayer? Like, can I just go in and pray by myself? I don't want to talk to anyone. I just want to be alone for some quiet time."

"Yes. It's open all day, most days. They've been doing that for a while, ever since our Helping Hands group took over the hall and kitchen to serve lunches."

"Who are the lunches for?"

"The homeless, Duncan, or whoever needs one."

"Oh," I bristled, embarrassed at my insensitivity.

"Don't you remember? We spoke about it before. You were thinking of volunteering with me. I try to go three times a week."

I'd sent a generous check instead and hadn't given it another thought. "Yes, Mom, sorry about that."

"No worries. Let me know if you reconsider. We can always use an extra set of hands, and I find it's very rewarding to help others."

I went the next day after spending the morning cleaning up my emails and returning a couple of calls. The church was about two miles from work, so I walked, taking my time and noticing the scenery. The village only has a non-denominational chapel and my Catholic roots always brought me back to my childhood church and parish. Dad's office is close to St. Mark's, and I thought about phoning to see if he was there and maybe grabbing a snack with him or a walk on the beach after my visit to the church. Even though two miles is a short distance, the differences are noticeable. The village area is manicured and always looks pristine. The location of St. Mark's, while a perfectly pleasant neighborhood, feels somewhat seedy in comparison.

The homes are still expensive, much higher than other areas, but you see occasional trash, maybe some graffiti or a loose dog or broken-down car, things that just are not common or tolerated in the village. Some homes need a fresh coat of paint. As I walked along, I made up asking prices for each one. Imagining I was selling them, practicing my pitch.

After a pleasant 40-minute walk, I arrived at St. Mark's church. The main entrance had sloped gradual steps and two lacy green trees on either side. It would have made a very symmetrical picture if there hadn't been a wheelchair ramp installed to the left. I wondered why disabled people couldn't just use the side entrance. I went in. No lights were on, but the stained glass windows, 7 on each side of the main aisle, provided a warm glow and a dapple of color on the shiny flooring. Under the windows were the Stations of the Cross, a series of 14 wood-carved scenes depicting the events of the Passion of Christ from his sentencing from Pontius Pilate to when he was put into the tomb. I was making my way down the aisle to the front nearer to the altar, my eyes focused on the stations when a hand reached out and grabbed my pant leg. A man was lying prone in the pew and had reached to grab me. It startled me. I swatted his hand away and jumped back.

"Hi Sinner," he drawled.

"Don't grab me! What are you doing here? You should leave," I snarled back, louder than I would have liked.

What the heck was a homeless person doing using the church as a napping place? So disrespectful. Then I looked around and saw several others stretched out on the benches, their plastic bags of belongings next to them. A woman wearing a sleek suit, kneeling in one of the front pews, turned to look at me, displeased to have her quiet time interrupted. "Shhhhhhhhh," she had a finger to her lips and was shaking her head in disapproval.

"Sorry," I whispered back, then noticed the man reaching with a dirt-stained hand for my leg again. He was lying in the shadows on the pew on his stomach, stretching his arm. It was creepy, like something you dream about. My body tensed up and recoiled from the man's touch. He smelled of something rotten and I thought I might gag.

"Look at me," he said, "You know me."

"I don't. Please let go," I hissed, trying to keep my voice low. "I'm leaving now," I offered, as if I owed this scumbag an explanation.

I walked out, maintaining my composure though I felt a surge of anger and was physically heated up. *Why in the world would the church sanction this? Was it allowed? Or did these people learn it was open, and they were taking advantage?* I walked in circles twice around the front steps, tugging at my hair, loosening my collar, and muttering to myself, before realizing that I could be mistaken for the crazy one by passersby. I was near Dad's office, so I continued in that direction, controlling my breath as I'd been taught by more than one therapist. I needed to get my heart rate down to think clearly. What was it that had gotten me so unhinged?

I arrived at the office of Knight, Sperry and Thomas and walked around the back. I was relieved to spot Dad's car. Hank came out of his doghouse in the small yard to greet me. I unlatched the little gate, walked through the yard on the decomposed granite path, and sat on the back stoop. I was glad Dad had brought Hank to work today, as he did most days. Shortly after we rescued Hank, Dad made him a yard in the back of the office. The office was originally an old Craftsman-style home, so the yard space was already there. It was simple, with grassy areas on the side, low bushes along the fence, a pathway to the back entrance, and a doghouse that matched the building in both color and style. Many of the properties on this street were mixed-use, offices, homes, or duplexes. Dad was concerned Hank might get lonely during the day if all three of us were out. Hank was, and is, a hit at the office and spends his time either stretched out on the sofa in the back room, greeting people at the door, begging for treats, lying under Dad's desk, or playing in his custom yard. As I sat, Hank pushed up next to me and positioned half his body on my lap. I buried my face in his fur and hugged him, then leaned back and called to my dad through the back screen door. He came right out.

"Hey, Duncan. What a pleasant surprise. Do you want to grab lunch or something?"

"Maybe just a glass of water. I'm gonna head back soon. I walked."

"Oh, good for you. It's such a nice day for a walk."

Hank had now heard the word "walk" twice and was looking expectantly at me. "Sure, boy. I'll take you," I said, scratching his golden head.

Dad lowered himself, knees cracking, and sat down next to me.

"Everything all right, Dunc? You seem a little shaken."

That's Dad, very perceptive. I suddenly didn't feel like re-hashing it. I just needed a glass of water and to leave. I was making a big deal out of nothing.

"No, I just forgot to bring water. I'm just thirsty. I'll have a glass, then head out. Okay if I take Hank?"

"Of course. You can't mention a you-know-what and then not take him. It'd be way too cruel. I'll grab his harness."

I downed a glass of cold water, used the restroom, leashed up Hank, then said goodbye to Dad and left. Hank and I made our way back to my office, taking a direction that did not pass the church. I wondered what had triggered me. Why was I so upset? Ever since I can remember, I have reacted viscerally when things don't go the way I think they should. I overheard my parents talking when I was in grade school, after a conference with my teachers. One of the teachers had described me as having an "over-inflated sense of self-importance." What a comment! She suggested I was spoiled, given too much, and lacked empathy for others. Teachers generally were not thrilled to have me in their class. My dad was adamant.

"They don't know what they're talking about. Duncan is just an energetic kid. And as for the rest. Nonsense, we can teach those things. He's just a kid. A good kid." Mom agreed. They always stood up for me and still do.

2005

I T'S 2005, AND TEN years have passed since that pivotal
moment of my life. I find it hilarious that the comic shop
is now a successful enterprise. Turns out, I was wrong about
it. The soft opening was not indicative of its future potential.
Good fortune for Hudson. He makes enough so Celeste
does not have to work and can stay home with their kids.
They had twins just about nine months after their wedding.
With word of mouth and the rise of the internet, the comic
shop was the perfect opportunity at the perfect time. Hudson
and his new partner were and are, wildly successful with no
hard feelings toward me. And why should they have any?
The whole thing was my idea. Knight's Comics. My name,
forever emblazoned on a shop I have no part in, and the
result of countless internet searches. Oh well. At least I did
my share to help contribute a place for lonely nerds to hang
out, trade comics, and role-play. I stop in occasionally and
to tell the truth, I'm uncomfortable. What else is new? I
guess there's just something about the way these people get
into the whole role-play thing. They take it so seriously.

Plus, why would I want to step into a created drama when I constantly have my own playing out in my head?

I continue to think about the night more often than I'd like, and almost daily, both by habit and necessity, I drive past where the incident occurred. For weeks after, I scoured news reports for missing persons, checked hospital records, death notices. There was nothing. I found the fire road that snaked through the side of the hill and walked it, searching. Logic tells me there is simply no way I hit someone, at least no proof. But, my gut, ten years later, still says something else. And the signs, if that's what they are, imaginary or not, keep plaguing me. I moved on with my life. I'm satisfied with my choice to enroll in Real Estate school, actually see it through, get my license and become a realtor, a very successful one. When I finished the coursework for my license, I traded in my old car. We hauled it to the junkyard for scrap, so the only evidence of the night is no longer around, except the couple of items only I know about hidden in my room. I thought that would calm me, and it did, a little. My newest car, my third since the night, another sleek black Lexus, is showy like the rest and hugs the road as I take those curves in the mountains above the ocean where I grew up and have decided to stay and continue my life.

In early June, I got an email from Martin's wife, Jane. I knew they were still together and had a kid, an 8-year-old girl, and they lived an hour away, having been given updates from Mom, who always knows the goings-on in everybody's lives. I did not respond or even open it. Then I got a message on my work phone from Jane. I returned it, thinking maybe she and Martin were ready to buy a house and wanted to use me as their agent. No, they wanted to set up a reunion, get all of us back together. Did I remember it had been 10 years since we had the weekend at Jane's parents? And already five years since Hudson's wedding in Cabo? I wondered why I was being included. Then Jane explained she was to sell her parents' house, so we could have it for the weekend just like 10 years ago. It would be a chance for us to recapture our youth one more time. Those who had kids and responsibilities could pretend they did not, just for a night. She wanted to give me the listing. I had to go. I explained I wouldn't stay the night, would just come Friday to say hello and look over the property. On Saturday morning, I had a meeting with a client. Not true, but a valid excuse. Part of me dreaded seeing my old friends. I'd made little effort to keep up with them since the Cabo trip, and every time I heard their names, I still thought only of that night. Whenever I occasionally see one in the village, I purposely appear flustered, as if I am in a hurry and have somewhere to be. I make a fast exit and later deal with the crushing aftermath of anxiety.

On the way to Jane's parents' house, I passed the spot I'd come to think of as *the place,* while driving in the opposite direction. I resisted the urge to turn the car around and pull over. Ten years and the feeling was still there. The prickle on my skin, like some supernatural force. The guilt. I wondered if I was a criminal, and I knew I'd never know. I pulled the car into the circular driveway and steeled myself for what was sure to be a long night. Everyone else must have arrived much earlier. My old friends were all there, plus a few others I didn't know.

Everyone was a little buzzed, and Travis had started a game of Beer Pong. I joined in and before I knew it, I was feeling lightheaded, but more importantly, I was having a genuinely good time. Why don't I spend more time with these people?

They really are fun. Saying I needed to find the facilities, I walked through the house taking notes on the small notepad I'd brought in my pocket, snapping photos with my digital camera, and counting bedrooms and bathrooms, estimating when the kitchen had last been remodeled, and considering the neighborhood's comparable sales. My commission for this house would be really nice and I already knew a few clients who might be interested. But for now, for once, I was going to let myself enjoy the night. And why not?

These were old friends.

After finishing up my wanderings, I made my way back to the main room, intending to continue playing Beer Pong. The lights were out, and the room was lit only by candles. The long table was pushed aside and a smaller, more intimate table for two was set up in the center of the room. The sofas were pushed up around the table and everyone was seated and hushed. How long had I been gone?

"Knight, come have a seat. She's about to start. Jane's going first."

"Fortune teller?" I whispered when I saw the lady seated at the table.

"No, she's a tarot card reader."

At this point, my mind is battling whether to claim an acute case of diarrhea and exit as quickly as possible, or stay and listen. One thing I was certain of, I would not be taking part.

Jane was directed to shuffle the cards until they "felt right." I released a scornful exhale and several sets of eyes locked on me.

I whispered, "Sorry." Were we honestly taking this seriously?

The tarot card lady took the deck and solemnly held the

cards. She was dressed in a dark purple sari with a black turban on her head for added effect. She directed Jane to focus on whatever it was she needed guidance on. Then she laid out cards in a pattern she referred to as the Seven Card Horseshoe Spread. She explained that in this configuration, the cards represent your past, your present, hidden influences, your overall self, the attitudes of others, what you should do about the situation, and what the likely outcome will be. I half listened with some interest, wondering if Jane's reading was so positive because the lady was her friend who was just learning the art of tarot reading and surely didn't want to upset her. She continued on, reading the fortunes of two more guests, who were very pleased and remarked at how accurate it seemed. At this point, I was planning my exit. I'd had enough.

"Why don't I read your cards next?" the lady asked me.

"Sure," I said. She handed me the deck. I shuffled the cards and calmly handed her the stack.

Card one, my past. She laid out the Tower card. I swear I heard her gasp a little. Card two, my present, was the Nine of Swords. Card three, hidden influences, was the Ten of Wands. Card four, we were now at the bottom of the horseshoe pattern and this was the card that supposedly represents me. She laid down The Moon. Card five, representing the influence of others, was the Nine of Pentacles card, and it was placed upside down. The sixth card was supposed to show the course of action I should take. It was the Queen of Cups. The last card was the Judgment card, representing the final outcome.

Until now, she had seemed confident; she was enjoying the attention. But after laying out the cards for me, she said, "You understand I don't really know what I'm doing yet. I'm just playing around, having fun, so don't necessarily take this to heart."

"Okay," I responded, and I took a picture with my digital camera. I'd always been fascinated by tarot cards, and figured I could study the photo later. The Tower card meant that an event from my past was negatively influencing my present and future. *You don't say?* I thought bitterly. The second card had a person with his head in his hands which meant something was bothering or worrisome to me or could mean there was something I needed to atone for. So far, the accuracy was startling and my discomfort grew.

"Anything you need to confess?" She eyed me and giggled nervously.

"Nope, I'm good." I said, trying to keep the sarcasm out of my voice. The Ten of Wands indicated I was weighed down by some kind of burden. For the Moon card, she referred to her notes and said it meant illusion or deception, that someone differs greatly from what they appear or may be hiding something.

I got even more uncomfortable, and my friends made a few cracks like, "Hey Knight, what are you hiding?"

"You sure you got nothing to confess? Are you guilty of a crime?"

"Wow, Knight's reading is a downer."

Lots of good-natured laughter ensued.

"Isn't there any good news? I don't think I want to have my cards read after all. I'd rather not know," Celeste remarked.

"Should I stop?" the reader asked and trembled, unsure. She was conspicuously not joining in the laughter of the others.

"No, continue," I said, "It's fascinating, truly," no longer attempting to hide the sarcasm. I wanted to know what the next cards supposedly meant. *Besides, how much worse could it get?*

She went on to say the fifth card meant success, achievement, and more than enough. However, it was reversed and therefore might mean a need for caution and discretion, or creating a lifestyle you don't want to maintain. The Queen of Cups foretold I should be more loving, honest, and compassionate, which made me feel as though I was currently none of those things. The last card, Judgement, pictured an angel with a yellow cloak which may as well have been a yellow raincoat, looking down on some poor wretched souls who were reaching skyward, indicating a reckoning or awakening, or, less serious, a time for some self-reflection.

So almost ten years ago to the hour, I found myself once again upset, feeling out of place and ostracized in the very same house. A reckoning. I needed to leave and went to grab my keys from the bowl on the way out back. I didn't mean to eavesdrop, but there was a group of women in the kitchen and I heard the tarot card reader say, "Who is that guy? I've never seen cards so dark. There was a lot of negative energy in the air. I'm really shaken up."

I did not take the route that passed the spot. Instead, I drove all the way downhill and came up the other side to go home. I did not need to pass the place tonight. I couldn't.

2006

I UPGRADED MY PHONE to the latest and greatest smart-
phone available, the Motorola gold RAZR. The gold is
a little flashy, but Ramon insists it's the one to have, and I
trust him in all things trendy. To have the internet at my
fingertips could be dangerous for me, so I held out until
now. My previous phone had the capability, but I only used
it for calls, occasional inferior-quality photos and to check
email once in a while. In my profession, it's important I
look the part of a successful realtor and having an expensive
car, wardrobe, and phone is part of the image. I never used
the camera on my old phone much. I preferred my digital
camera, but the quality of this one is so much better. I gave
myself the name *Hanxbro* on my new account and started
experimenting with the search tools, quickly realizing how
folks get hooked on their phones. I hadn't understood the
capabilities and potential for mental distraction.

"How fast do you need to drive to kill a pedestrian?" I typed
in.

The answer came up as 25 to 35 miles per hour depending

on how much bodily contact there is. A person could survive a hit at these speeds too, depending on individual circumstances. I kept scrolling through the results of my initial search and clicking on related links, which led to a site where people were discussing ways to successfully commit crimes. Then I entered a chat room, figuring I could lurk as a fly on the wall and maybe learn something useful. Individuals with names like "GetawyWithit" and "PrfctCrm" commented on how to hide a body and how to destroy evidence. Theoretically, of course.

Then a message popped up on my screen, "SO what do you think, Hanxbro? What are you covering up? Need help with hiding a body?" I almost threw my phone down. *How were these people contacting me? How had they seen my name?*

Was Hanxbro linked to my true identity? Seized with paranoia, I powered down my phone and was too afraid to turn it on for the rest of the day.

I knocked softly, then entered Ramon's office. He was sitting in his desk chair, leaning back with his feet up on his desk, staring at his phone. He glanced up when I walked in.

"How do you like the new phone, Dunc? It's great, huh? I love mine."

"Yeah. I like it. Hey, I wanted to ask you, when you go into a chat room, do people know who you are? Can they access your identity?"

"Not really. They'll just see the name you go by, I think. So, you're going into some shady chat rooms, huh?" He laughed. "Looking at porn and don't want to get caught? Or are you stalking someone?"

"No. Nothing too exciting. More like I don't want someone stalking me," I improvised.

"Oh, like an old girlfriend. I get it. You don't want her

seeing you on a new dating site. Is that it?"

"Sure, something like that." *If only it was that innocuous.*

"Man, I've been there. I had to change my number and my personal email to get away from this one chick. It was getting to be too much how she always found me."

"Anyway, other than that, the phone is great. Thanks for hooking me up."

"No problem."

I backed out of Ramon's office and decided I was done with work for the day. Even though I risked missing calls, I was still not ready to turn my phone on. I hadn't bothered setting up voicemail yet. I got in my car and sat, staring at my phone on the passenger seat where I'd tossed it, regretting that I bought it. I needed a distraction, so I drove over to Knight's Comics to see if Hudson was in. A parking place was available right out front. The store is in the middle of the block in an old brick building. I stared up at the giant sign of "Knight's Comics" painted on an eight-foot rectangle of black metal with red lettering outlined in gold hanging over the old brick facade. Some of the paint on the sign is chipping, but that only makes it look cooler and more vintage. I pushed open half of the heavy oak double door and let my eyes adjust. Inside the shop, the walls and carpet are black, but it's not too dark in the room. Glass display cases hold first editions and older copies of comics while spinning turnstiles hold new, less expensive ones. I used to be so into comics and role-playing games, but as soon as I opted out of the store ownership, my interest waned. A pegboard on the wall has playing cards for interactive games.

There are shelves with various figurines and posters in hard plastic that you can flip through in bins. Other shelves hold stacked t-shirts and caps and merchandise like purses, lunch boxes, and mugs. Small spinners have necklaces and earrings, key chains, stickers, and lanyards. So it's not strictly comic books, it's much more. I'm impressed with the way it turned out. Hudson was better off without me.

The major draw though is the game tables. Each circular table seats up to six players.

Customers can bring their own cards or rent them along with the table. They can reserve ahead or just show up. The tables rent for $30/hour and are always full, sometimes with the same group for hours at a time. It was 4:30. Older teens and young guys in their twenties occupied five of the six gaming tables. The players hunched over their cards as they focused on whatever magical fantasy was playing out. I walked over and asked, to no one in particular, "Hey, does anyone know if Hudson's around?" Sets of eyes shot daggers at me. How dare I interrupt their concentration? One kid pointed at me and whispered something unintelligible to his seatmate. I felt like they were all looking at me.

"Sorry. Didn't mean to disturb your game," I offered a weak apology.

"Sure, Old Man. Whatever."

Old Man?! My anger and frustration peaked. I grabbed the little punk by the neck of his shirt. *I'll show you who's an Old Man.*

"What did you call me? You little twerp?" As soon as the words came out, I let go of the kid's shirt, horrified at my reaction. What was wrong with me? Embarrassment took over.

"Hey!" the boy shouted.

"Just kidding," I tried to cover for myself, "But seriously, I'm 33. Hardly old!" I defended, forcing a laugh as I took a step back.

Hudson walked in then from the back of the store.

"Hey, Knight. What's up? Everything ok here? I saw you on the camera from my office." I wasn't sure what to say.

"Knight?" the kid at the table asked.

"Yeah, that's right. This guy's name is the inspiration for Knight's Comics. I hope you're showing him proper respect," Hudson said.

"Well, that was a long time ago," I added lamely, "now I sell real estate." As if any of these punks cared what I did.

"Yes. We know," one teenage boy snickered.

"Come on back. You got time for a beer?"

I wished I hadn't come in, but I followed Hudson to his office. He was already pulling out two beers from his fridge. I accepted one and held the cold glass up to my forehead before popping off the cap and taking a gulp. Hudson was wearing worn-out jeans with a rip in one knee and a black character t-shirt that had bleach spots. He had on flip-flops. In contrast, I wore custom-tailored linen slacks, a designer short-sleeved golf shirt, and handmade leather loafers, actually fairly California casual, but still professional. No wonder those kids thought I was a joke, the antithesis of teenage cool. Fresh embarrassment surfaced.

Why did I come here? I was feeling anxious about the chat room and afraid of being discovered. I took another long swig of beer and set down the bottle. *Just act natural.*

"How are you and Celeste doing? Married life good? What about the twins?" As I asked, I racked my brain to remember the twins' names. How could I forget their names?

"Oh, Ethan and Nathan are great. They just started playing soccer. It's pretty fun to watch a bunch of five-year-olds chase the ball around." Right, so they're Ethan and Nathan, Ethan and Nathan. I need to get better with names.

89

"I remember when we played. We were pretty little too. It was all about the snacks. I can't believe you're a dad now."

"It's the best, Knight. The best. If you ever want to come watch, we'd love to have you. It's hilarious. Being a dad lets me relive my childhood."

"Yeah, maybe I will." I knew it wasn't likely. "Hey, how's Celeste? I haven't seen her in a while."

"She's great." Hudson was grinning from ear to ear. "She's such a wonderful mom." He lowered his voice and added, "Only a few people know yet, but we're expecting another baby." The happiness on Hudson's face was clear. I could not relate, but I wanted to.

"Wow. Hud, congratulations. I can't believe you'll be a father of three. And it looks like the shop is doing really well. I see your ads everywhere. And your commercials."

"It's very lucrative, yes. I just bought out my partner, so it's all mine. Investors approached me about franchising too, but I'm not sure. We'll see."

"It's got the best name."

"Definitely," he laughed, "all for the best. How's the real estate gig? Are you still loving it? I see your signs everywhere."

"I'm doing well. Most of my sales are in the Village, so yeah, I'd say I'm doing quite well."

"Good. Great. I always knew you would. How about your love life? Are you dating anyone?"

"No, too busy, I guess. I don't know. Maybe I should think about it. I'm not getting any younger."

"Celeste might know someone to set you up with. A blind date?"

"I'll let you know. Maybe I'll try one of those dating sites or something." I knew there was exactly a zero percent chance that would happen. I think I would like to meet someone, but the practicalities of going about it are more than I will explore. If it ever happens, it will be natural. There is just no way I could join a site or get set up on a date. Hudson and I chatted for a while longer. I finished my beer, declined a second, said goodbye, and left.

I sat in my car for a minute, then picked up my phone where I'd left it on the passenger seat. I powered it on and stared at it. I decided then and there it would be for calls, checking email, and sending messages to clients and people I knew. I would no longer use it as a search tool, and would absolutely not be going to any questionable websites, and definitely not dating ones.

2007

I 'VE NEVER BELIEVED I was popular, even during high
school, and I know I'm not now, at least in the sense that
people seek me out to spend time with me socially. And yet,
every time I opened my email, a list of invitations to join
Facebook greeted me. Some names I didn't even recognize.
Some were clients, and some I swear were from Junior High.
I did not want to go down the rabbit hole, but everyone
seemed to be joining and according to my office secretary,
we should have an account for the office and add "Find us
on Facebook" to every business card and advertisement.

All right. I signed up for the benefit of the office. Next, I
needed a profile picture. Luckily, every few years we have a
photographer come to the office and take portraits for our
business cards and ads. Yup, that's my mug on bus benches
throughout the village, the whole county, and sometimes on
the actual side of a bus, but thankfully not on the side of a
portable toilet like Joe the insurance man. That is where I
draw the line. It's quite dignified. Especially when kids draw
boogers out of my nose, or give me glasses or a blacked-out

tooth. I find it pretty comical, to be honest. What isn't funny is when I see "Killer" written under my name in block letters. The first time I noticed, I was shaken. Kids just do dumb stuff. But why my picture? Why Killer? I swear this paranoia is going to kill me. My nerves can't take it sometimes.

Once I officially signed up for Facebook, I was inundated with friend requests from people I'd known in the past: clients, friends of friends, acquaintances, relatives, and some people for whom I had no clue what the connection might be. There were very few actual friends, as I said, I don't have many, and this seemed only to be highlighted with my joining Facebook. I kept my account and profile strictly professional, only posting real estate-related information like new listings or house-hunting tips. It initially surprised me to see posts about people's morning cappuccino and other inane things. Maybe my not caring explains my lack of friendships. Before I knew it wasn't expected, I responded with a short greeting whenever someone sent a friend request. Just a "Hi, nice to hear from you." I didn't even know that this was not what you do, and it only makes people think you are weird, until overhearing the girl who works at the front desk having a conversation with one of the junior agents.

"Oh, my God. Can you even believe how lame and awkward it is when random people send you messages?"

"I know. I just ignore them. So awkward."

I had to ask. "But don't you expect a response if you send them a friend request?"

The red-haired one responded, "Um, no." And I swear she rolled her eyes at me. There was a solid chance I'd sent both girls a greeting. Why am I so inept socially?

I confirmed this with Ramon, who said people just wanted

to increase their friend count as some kind of personal validation, and no one expects or wants to actually communicate with you.

"So, how many friends do you have?" I asked him.

He seemed a little defensive and answered, "Well, I have 342, but I don't really care or keep up with it. It's just for work connections, you know? How many friends do you have Knight, excluding me, of course?"

"I only have 46 so far," I said.

Ramon let out a hearty laugh. "Oh, Knight. You are such a stud!"

"Sure, Ramon. Glad I could give you a laugh."

So when Julia Howard sent a request, I clicked "accept" and thought nothing of it. I did not send her a "Hello."

She was a serial poster, constantly writing about funny things that happened in her class with her students (she's a teacher), posting pictures of her cats (she has three), or a hike she'd done. I always inspected everything she posted and found myself somewhat stalking her page. I was interested, which was new for me. I never saw a man in any of her photos and none was ever mentioned. There did not seem to be any one particular female either. This kindled a hope in me that possibly she was single.

"Hey, Mom, any idea of where my old yearbooks are?" I knew she would know, and she did. Mom pulled them off the shelf in the library, where they were kept in perfect date order.

"Honey, did you want high school or elementary, or all of them?" She asked.

"Let's start with high school," I said.

"I'll bring them to the dining room table and go through them with you. Are you looking for someone in particular?"

She carried the stack of four high school yearbooks and plopped them on the table.

"Well, I just joined Facebook, and I'm trying to figure out how I know someone who friended me. It's this new computer thing, Mom. You probably haven't heard of it."

"Duncan, of course I've heard of it. I joined last year. All my friends are on, and a bunch of your old chums from high school sent me friend requests, which of course I accepted. I'm setting Dad's business up with a page, too. I was going to ask you if you wanted me to do a real estate page for you. It's a lot of fun. I love seeing what people are up to."

Mom was apparently way ahead of me. I handed her a yearbook.

"We're looking for Julia Howard," I said. "She's the one who I am trying to figure out how I know her. I'm guessing it's high school."

"Here she is." My mom had my sophomore yearbook and pointed to a picture of Julia as a ninth grader. Julia was one grade behind me. Her name was the same, so either she had never married, or she had gotten a divorce, I reasoned. I'd never seen children in her Facebook photos, only her friends' kids and sometimes her students, always with their faces obscured for privacy. We may have had a class together in high school, but I wasn't sure. Her high school photos showed a girl with large owl-like glasses who was in Latin Club and Key Club and Honor Society. I knew I would not have paid attention to her then. I felt a little bad about it, if I'm being honest.

"Let me see a picture of her now," my mom requested. I pulled up her profile on Facebook.

"She's quite pretty, Duncan. Are you planning to ask her out, maybe?"

This is what I love about Mom. We have never had a conversation about me dating or my love life at all. Ever. She never prods for information, and wasn't now. She was just being supportive.

"Yes, Mom. I think I will ask her out."

"I think that would be lovely."

As I hatched a plan to contact Julia without seeming obvious, she made the first move. She responded to a post I'd made about tips on finding the best-fit home for your lifestyle. Her comment said, "Hi Duncan, I'm actually considering purchasing my first home. Do you mind if I call your office and ask you a few questions?"

"Absolutely, yes. I would be happy to help you. Call any time." I responded immediately with my office phone number. She called the next afternoon. She sounded nervous.

"Hi Duncan, do you remember me from high school? I was a grade below you."

"Of course, I remember. You were in the Latin Club right?" How would I know this unless I looked her up? What a stupid thing to say. Good thing she was not in person to witness my face turning every shade of red. I stood up and closed my office door and shut the blinds.

"Yes, I was, but we had World Civ together when I was in 10th grade. You were in 11th. You had to repeat it right? Oh God, I'm sorry. What a thing to say. I didn't mean.."

"It's fine. You're right. I had to repeat it. The first time, I failed the class. I blame the teacher. He was super boring. I graduated though, on time, too." I laughed to put her at ease before asking, "So, what can I help you with?"

"Well, I'm interested in buying a mobile home. There's this great little park near my school with one for sale by the owner. I'm sure this isn't the type of house you're used to selling, but I don't know any other realtors."

How could I convey that this was a terrible idea without insulting her? I felt like she deserved better. Mobile homes were never a smart financial investment. Plus, I couldn't picture Julia living in one, no matter how nice. I know I'm biased from selling multi-million dollar properties, but still.

"What city?" I knew it was Paula Serra, just as I knew what school she worked at and what grade she taught, though I could not very well admit it. For any other potential client, I would have stopped the conversation and said I don't cover that area, but maybe I can recommend another agent. My focus is exclusively Ocean View Village and my clients have millions to spend.

"It's Paula Serra. I don't know if it's the best idea, but I feel like I should try to purchase something. I have a little money saved. My parents passed away rather suddenly, and I finally paid off my student loans and I feel like I'm a little ahead for the first time ever. Sorry, I'm rambling."

"No, you're fine. I'm really sorry to hear about your parents. Hey, would you maybe want to meet at Village Coffee? We could catch up and I could answer any questions, run some numbers… or of course you can come to the office if you feel more comfortable." I seriously wanted to kick myself right about now. I sounded like an idiot.

"I'd love to meet for coffee. Would Saturday at 10 work for you?"

I had a showing at 10 but decided I would move it. I would not pass up this opportunity. "Definitely, Saturday is great. See you at 10."

My body felt light. I was smiling. I leaned back in my chair and enjoyed the moment.

Saturday at 9:55 am I watched Julia park her car, a faded,

compact, red Toyota. She pulled down the mirror and applied lipstick, blotting her lips on a scrap of paper, before getting out. The wind blew her hair, and she tucked it behind her ear and hunched up her oversized bag onto her shoulder. Realizing I was holding my breath, I forced myself to let it out. *Try to relax. You meet clients all the time. This is no different.* But it felt different. She walked in, not noticing me at first, and went straight to the counter. Then she half turned, scanning the few tables, spotted me, waved at me, and called out, "Hey, I'm just gonna grab a coffee and muffin. Do you want anything?"

"Nah, I'm good, thanks."

Julia approached with her coffee and muffin, setting them down and dropping her large bag on the floor. I hoped I didn't appear as nervous as I felt. I stood up.

"It's great to see you. It's been years." She held out her hand, and I shook it lightly. It was warm and cool at the same time.

I made eye contact and surprised myself by saying, "I'm really glad you called me. I was actually trying to come up with a reason to get in touch with you and then..."

She interrupted, "I came up with a reason and saved you the hassle, right?"

"Right. I mean, no, not right."

"I know what you mean," she looked at me, her eyes mischievous.

"So, can I answer any questions about the home you want to purchase? I contacted the listing agent and we can get in today if you want."

Not wanting her to sense my nervousness, I picked up my coffee and took a sip, needing something to occupy my hands. Even though I knew purchasing this property was a poor investment, it still provided a perfect reason to spend time with Julia. I could figure out later how to steer her away from actually buying it.

"Yes. Let's go look at it. I'd like to see the inside if you're sure you can spare the time," Julia said.

"I have no other commitments today," I responded. "We can take as long as you need."

And that is how my relationship with Julia began, who I think it is fair to say is the love of my life. I did not know I was missing something until I met her. And I already feel like I can not live without her. But let me back up. We went to the mobile home she was thinking of buying. I drove, secretly hoping she'd be impressed by my Lexus. The property was in a small park with around 20 other mobile homes, some newer, some ancient, and in disrepair. The one we looked at was in decent shape but was overpriced, and the space rent was too high as well.

Julia explained, "It's not that I love it or anything. It's more like I feel like I'm supposed to be at a place in my life where I own a place. I actually love where I live now. It's close by. Do you want to see it?"

"Sure, that will help me understand your taste. Then maybe I can help you find something more suitable. But Julia, I have to confess here. I am not one to advocate doing anything because you think you're supposed to. For example, I still live with my parents. Should I move out and get my own place? That's what society prescribes, but I'm happy there. I have the funds to move, but I just don't want to. Maybe you don't want to move either. For what it's worth, I say if you are happy where you are, stay. You only have yourself to answer to. Who cares what anyone else thinks?"

She thanked me for being honest, then we drove over to her place. She lives in a tiny house on a ranch. At one point, it was a caretaker's house. To get there, we needed to go through the main gate, which must be opened and closed by hand so none of the cows can walk out. The property owners have a variety of farm animals and an area used by the local 4H kids to raise their animals. They are hobby farmers, growing whatever they want and selling the excess at the Farmer's Market or donating it to the local food banks.

Julia's house is a tidy little cottage, set apart from the primary residence, and it looks straight out of a fairy tale. It has old worn wood floors, a stone fireplace in the main area, a small kitchen, and a bedroom. The door off the kitchen leads to a 4 seasons room that Julia calls the "catio" because it's where her 3 cats spend most of their time. When I first saw the cats, I thought about Hank. And my thought was that I would need to get him used to cats.

We took one of the ATVs and explored the property. Julia impressed me with her skill in maneuvering through pastures and even crossing a small creek, and soon we were as comfortable as old friends and were laughing like we were kids again. Afterward, Julia made us some lunch. We ate it in the catio and I felt a sense of home, like I was just where I needed to be. One cat even sidled up to me and allowed me to stroke its head. Later, I drove Julia back to her car.

"Are you free tomorrow?" I didn't feel like waiting a few days to ask.

"Yes. What do you have in mind?"

"A hike and a swim?"

"Definitely, yes."

We have been together ever since. I never felt like something was missing before Julia, but it was.

2008

M<small>Y NEWEST PROPERTY SHOWING</small> was a success. Pretty sure I nailed it, so I walked to Village Coffee for an Americano and an orange scone. I was running the numbers in my head and wondering if I should start the paperwork. I rarely do this out of superstition, but after seeing the prospective buyers' reactions, I was all but sure the deal would go through. Money would not be an issue. The couple was pre-approved. The only possible snag was the inspection; structural damage or another pricey fix would occasionally cause a buyer to back out, but rarely. Real estate in the hills above the village is white hot and people will pay almost anything, 3.2 million for this one. Add to the fact that there is essentially a moratorium on new builds, and existing inventory is extremely limited. Folks tend to hang on to their properties here. Also, where else are you going to get acreage, an ocean view, privacy and perfect weather?

I entered the coffee shop and noticed a sheriff seated in the corner. He had set his radio on the little cafe table and was picking at a donut while scrolling through his phone.

I laughed to myself at the stereotype-come-to-life. He was middle-aged, wearing a beige uniform, dark hair shorn in a short crew cut, graying at the temples. Must be on a break.

"Don't do it!" I told myself as my body walked over to him.

"Hi Sir. Thanks for your service to our community." Could I have sounded like a bigger douche?

"It's always nice to be appreciated," he responded, looking up from his phone to study me.

"Of course."

"Aren't you the big time real estate agent?"

"Not big time, but, yes, Knight, Duncan Knight of Village Real Estate. Is there anything I can help you with real estate-wise?"

"Nah, our graffiti team sure stays busy cleaning the 'Killer' messages off your bench ads though," he chuckled at his own joke.

"Yeah, well, it's great to be famous, I guess." *Seriously? What am I supposed to say?*

"Any suspects? On the graffiti?"

"No, we figure it's high schoolers trying to be funny."

"Makes sense," I said, recalling how I'd offended those boys in the comic shop. *Would they have the wherewithal to carry a grudge and seek retribution by defacing my photo?* Doubtful. Since we were already engaged in conversation, I figured I'd pick his brain a little. Why not?

"I've been reading a lot of crime novels lately and so often everything is wrapped up perfectly in the end. Is that usually how it goes?"

"Depends," he said. "The devil is in the details, so to speak. Sometimes it's very easy to connect the dots. People think they can get away with committing crimes. I'm here to tell you, they rarely do." He took a bite of donut and leaned back in his chair, his belt straining to contain his considerable girth. I couldn't help but wonder how he'd do on a foot chase of a suspect.

"Are there many unsolved crimes here in town? If you're able to answer."

"Other than the matter of the Killer graffiti perpetrator? No, not too many. It's a pretty low-key area as far as crime is concerned."

"Are there any missing persons? It seems like a person could go missing on purpose and if no one wanted to find them, like if they had no family, it'd be fairly easy to disappear, don't you think?" Was I rambling? Being obvious?

"If they went far enough away, and no one cared to look, then yes, they could 'disappear', but if they are known, or missed or are wanted for a crime, they'll be found, eventually. You can't hide forever." He paused again for a sip of his coffee, then continued, "Sometimes, it's the opposite. We find a body and do not know who it is until a relative or someone can identify the person."

"Really? Does that happen often? I mean, are there very many unclaimed dead people?"

"No. It's not common. But we did just have a woman claim a body, her own husband. She and another homeless man said the deceased's name was Barton Miller. Of course, we'll have to verify that with records and such. But, apparently, he was a local transient, probably about your age, but looked older. They always do. It's a rough life."

"Barton Miller? We went to school together as kids. It must be the same guy. I never knew what happened to him after high school." I felt sad and shocked that he was dead.

"It's a tragedy. He was a junkie. I'd see him around town, then he'd disappear. His wife, if she was his wife, said they lived in the dry river bottom with a group. There's a whole encampment there. We keep moving them out, but they keep coming back. My partner found the deceased in the bushes when we were doing a sweep of the area during community clean-up day over the weekend. Appears to be an overdose, practically inevitable with that lot."

"That is truly sad. What a waste." *What else could be said?*

The talkative officer never specifically answered my question about missing persons in this area, and I could not very well ask again without seeming obvious, but I wanted to continue the conversation.

"At what point is a missing person presumed dead? Is it a certain amount of time or is an actual body required?"

"Well, to definitively say there would have to be a body. Until then, we never can truly know."

"Sure. I understand. Thanks for chatting with me, officer. Please have another coffee. It's on me. Have a nice day."

"Thanks. You as well. The name's Shiloh, by the way, Sheriff Shiloh. Don't hesitate to call, if you need anything," he said, handing me his card. I paid the cashier and deposited a tip in the jar. As I left, I saw him go back to looking at his phone.

I returned to my office but had a hard time focusing. Barton Miller was dead. I should feel sad, but I didn't. I didn't know him anymore, hadn't been in contact since, what, 6th grade? He was just someone from my past. I wondered though, if I hadn't rejected him so harshly when we were kids, is it possible his life would have turned out differently? I felt guilty. I needed to see Julia. She is like a balm. She makes everything better. I knew she was still teaching, but I sent her a text.

"Hey, if you're not busy, do you want to come over for

dinner?" She responded immediately.

"Already planning on it. Ha ha. Your dad and I are going to watch the season premiere of Real True Crime."

This made me laugh. My parents love Julia as much as I do and have no boundaries about planning their own activities with her.

"Great. I'll third wheel it with you and Dad then."

She sent a laughing emoji and the message, "See you at 6."

Julia was already at the house when I arrived, her silver hatchback parked next to the garage. I'd given her the car for her birthday. I chose it carefully, knowing she would be reluctant to accept it. In the end, she agreed she needed something reliable. I tossed my briefcase on my bed, stripped out of my office clothes in favor of lounge pants, a t-shirt, and slides then joined the three of them on the patio deck. Dad was at the barbeque grilling tri-tip. Mom had made a big salad and Julia was preparing the garlic bread to broil when the meat was finished. Her chestnut hair was in a ponytail and she was dressed in gray sweatpants and a t-shirt from our old high school. She always changed clothes after work. I smiled as I walked over to give her a hug. Hank was patiently hanging out at Dad's side, hoping some meat would come his way.

"Julia said you might join us for Real True Crime, Dunc. It's the season premiere."

"I might. I'm not really into crime shows, though. Light comedy is what I prefer. You know that, Dad."

"Yup. Glad I've got a fellow fan now," he gestured toward Julia, "Mom doesn't like it either."

This mutual interest was one reason Julia and Dad had bonded immediately. Then she took one look at his library and I'm lucky he was already married. After dinner and two games of Hearts with Julia and my parents, I stuck around and joined Dad and Julia for the premiere of their favorite show. I settled on the couch with Julia on one side and Hank on the other. Dad was reclined in his favorite leather chair, his worn-out slippers on his feet, and a large bowl of popcorn balanced in his lap. Mistake. In the introduction, the host explained with all the necessary drama how this particular criminal had evaded capture for over 13 years. Everyone: parents, extended family, friends, and coworkers believed he was a righteous guy, when in his spare time, he was racking up kills.

I stayed throughout the first segment, then stood up and said, "Ok, I'm out. You two enjoy the rest." I gave Julia a quick kiss and headed out to the pool house. Hank followed me, began barking, then ran around the back of the pool house.

"What is it Hank? Are the raccoons back?" I hoped it was raccoons and not a skunk.

Hank had been skunked once and hopefully had learned his lesson, but I doubted it.

"Come, Hank come!" I yelled out to him. When he didn't obey, I trudged around back to see what he was up to. He was sitting under the bedroom window. I shined the light from my phone and didn't see any critters. I aimed it down and saw boot prints on the soft ground near Hank. There were smudges on the window. Did Hank make those with his snout? He gave a couple of sharp barks, ran into the bushes, then came right back to me. I walked to the bushes and shined the light. I heard rustling from far away on the property. Nothing unusual. There are all kinds of animals who live around here, coyotes, deer, raccoons, skunks, and bobcats, even the occasional black bear or cougar. It's practically wilderness. I'm sure the boot prints were from the gardeners. They come every week and were probably trimming the bushes.

Too tired to explore further, I went inside. The door wasn't locked. *Had I locked it?*

Something felt off. The smell of damp earth was subtle but present. I felt compelled to check my "evidence." The piece of fabric and fortune cookie fortune was safe and sound in the back of my sock drawer. My nerves calmed as I thoughtfully questioned what significance the items would have to anyone but me? My journal, which I'd taken to wedging between the bed and the nightstand, I'm sure, remained hidden. Just one more thing to check, the jacket. I stepped into the walk-in closet and noticed it in a heap on the floor on top of my shoes. I grabbed it. Was it damp? It felt moist. I hung it back up. I was shaking now and was sure I'd find that someone had tampered with my journal. No, still hidden. I sat at my desk with my head in my hands, my elbows resting on my ink blotter calendar. Did I need to be concerned? Should I be? I looked down at the calendar and saw a smudge of dried mud. Hank sometimes jumps up and leans his paws on the desk to see out the window. He must have caused this and the window smudges, too. That was a reasonable, rational explanation. The jacket fell. A jacket could easily be jostled off the hanger when I moved around other clothes or hung something up. I just didn't notice it earlier. The pool house often felt a little damp.

I waited until the show ended, 9 pm, and went back to the main house, locking my door behind me. I kissed Julia and said good night, and when she left, I put on the percolator with some dark roast coffee. I knew there would be no sleep tonight. My mind would ruminate on the past and I would watch a mental movie in an unending loop until I could distract myself with work the next day.

2009

M Y PROPOSAL TO JULIA was just right. I wasn't aware it was going to happen, but a sparkle in the jewelry store caught my eye and before I knew it, I had paid $31,000 for a beautiful braided rose gold band with a large round cut diamond flanked by two round tanzanite stones on either side. I would never let her know it cost about the same as her car. Once I had the ring, it was inevitable.

Saturday morning, she met me at my house at 9 to hike up to the waterfall. We like to go before it's too crowded and the heat sets in. I stashed the ring in the small pocket of my daypack. The bigger pouch held a thin towel, some trail mix and some water. It was technically fall, but as usual and typical of coastal California, it hadn't cooled off yet. The air was feeling a little more crisp; the sky was that brilliant fall blue and the leaves of the Oaks along the trail were just beginning to shed, making a pleasant crunch under our feet and a fun place for Hank to do some off-leash sniffing. I wanted to remember everything about the day.

"So do you think I can convince your mom to make some

crafts or pumpkin breads or something to donate to our Fall Harvest Festival at school?" Julia asked.

"Yes, of course. You know she lives for that sort of thing," I replied. "And do you want to marry me?"

Julia stopped and looked at me. Her hair was pushed back by a headband and was gathered into a ponytail. Her face was fresh with no makeup, her oversized sunglasses shaded her eyes.

"It sounded like you just asked me to marry you," she said.

"Yes, I did," I said casually, but not able to hide an enormous goofy grin.

"Well then, yes, I would love to."

"I have something for you," I said, unzipping the pocket of my backpack. "Take a look." I placed the ring box in her hand. She pushed her sunglasses on top of her head, opened it, and gasped.

"How did you? When did you? This is the most beautiful ring I have ever seen."

"I don't know. I saw it and just knew. I'm glad you like it."

"Isn't it too much, though?"

"Never." I slipped it on her finger and it was a perfect fit.

Even Hank seemed to get in on the excitement when I told him Julia was officially going to be his mom.

We continued to the waterfall, took our shoes off, and put our feet in the stream. Julia was eager to get back to the house to tell my parents the news. She kept looking at the ring and at me. I think she was pretty shocked that I'd gotten the nerve to ask.

"I can't believe they don't know. Duncan, how did you keep this from your mom? She's so intuitive, I'm surprised she didn't figure it out."

"Well, I just bought the ring yesterday, and I've been

avoiding eye contact since. Even so, I suspect they know something's up."

Julia already knew my parents loved her dearly, and she felt the same.

Mom and Dad were ecstatic, and I suspect relieved I would not be a forever bachelor. Sometimes I think they love Julia even more than they love me. And I am okay with that. Julia and Mom got straight to work planning the wedding. I insisted on a small, intimate affair, and they agreed. It would be a church ceremony followed by a luncheon reception at the Village Women's Club. The month of June would work best, so Julia could be on summer break. I planned our Hawaiian honeymoon, a beachside villa with a private pool.

We discussed if we should get our own place, but decided, at least for now, we would join my parents in the big house and move into the second master suite. My parents offered to remodel it however we liked, as one of our wedding gifts. I left the details to Julia. My childhood bedroom would become a den for us or a home office, and we would keep the two remaining bedrooms for guests. Dad had his library and Mom her craft room, which were Julia's favorite rooms in the house and which both parents were eager to share with her. We would all share the common areas of the family room, living room, dining room, sun porch, and kitchen. After so many years, the pool house would become just a pool house again.

The wedding was a whirlwind. The day seemed to fly by so quickly. I met Julia at the church at 10 for the ceremony. She was stunning in an antique white lace dress. Her hair was up in the front, with long curls in the back. Saturday, June 6. Pictures followed, and then the reception. Most of my office mates attended, the ones I consider friends, Herb and Margie and some other former clients-turned-friends, and my usual childhood buddies, all thrilled that after all these years, the old man, me, finally took the plunge. Some of them are already divorced now and remarried to a new spouse. But I am me. I do things in my own way and in my own time.

Julia had her close girlfriends and friends from work. My parents had quite a time narrowing their guest list, particularly my Mom, being that she is a friend to all.

True to their word, Mom and Julia kept the reception simple, pasta dishes and light salads with cupcakes for dessert. White wine and a champagne toast, no open bar. Simple fresh flowers in clear vases on each table, with white linen tablecloths. No DJ, but there was a small band.

Most importantly for me, other than the first dance, I was not to be put in the spotlight. Hudson gave a gracious toast, and so did Dad. Julia tossed her bouquet and Adriene from my office caught it. By all accounts, the day went smoothly, perfectly.

We stayed the night in town at the cozy Village Inn and took a limo to the airport the next morning. We had a direct flight to Hawaii, sitting in first-class seats. That was another gift from Mom and Dad. I felt calm and content, completely secure in my decision to marry Julia, and I could not keep the smile from my face. There is no one else I've ever felt so complete with. Julia is my person. The flight was smooth and upon arrival, locals greeted us with plumeria leis.

When we picked up the rental car, the gentleman on duty upgraded it to an off-road convertible Jeep. He smiled and said, "Someone told me it's your honeymoon." When we arrived at our villa, there was chilled champagne and chocolate-dipped strawberries, and two dozen red roses in a crystal vase. A note said there were reservations for that evening at the steak house on the beach. In addition, we had vouchers for a couple's massage, and a sunset cruise, all arranged by my mom. She had outdone herself again.

"Julia, I hope you don't feel like my mom is too much. Believe me, she only wants the best for us. She won't meddle in our lives."

"Duncan, I love your parents. I don't feel that way at all about your mom. And you should probably know, she asked my permission before booking any of these things for us."

"Ah, yes. I should have known."

"The snorkeling excursion is all Dad's idea, though. And he wants to get credit for it," she laughed, "I'm so glad we found each other, and I feel like I have parents again too, who I couldn't love more. Oh, and also Hank, best dog ever."

"Well, you know if Hank didn't like you, I never could have married you," I said, only half joking.

We settled into a week of a balance of activities and luxuriating rest. On both Monday and Tuesday, we lazed on the lanai for breakfast, then took a swim, went for a hike, and discovered a new beach. Wednesday, we were scheduled for the snorkeling excursion. I jolted awake, sweaty in the night, and instinctively checked the clock: 1 AM. Of course, I would wake up near the time of the incident. I got out of bed and walked out to the patio, careful not to disturb Julia. Would I ever be able to share this demon with her? I waited for 1:35 to pass before returning to bed.

In the morning, a slight headache settled in. I took two aspirin with my coffee. The date was in the back of my mind, as it always is, but a busy day distracted by the one I love was the best way to spend it. The snorkeling was spectacular. We reached out to the fish with frozen peas. I felt the smoothness of their bodies as they brushed against my hands and torso. It was only us and one family on the boat, so we didn't have to deal with any crowds. The family of four was charming, the children adorable and chatty, and I sensed a longing in Julia. We are both hoping to have a child of our own. The captain eased the boat into a protected cove offshore. It was a less visited location, and we had it to ourselves. Visibility was excellent for snorkeling or just watching the sea life from above. He had suggestions for activities for the rest of our stay.

"Have you seen the cliff divers yet?" he asked.

"No, where do we do that?" Julia wanted to know.

"They dive multiple times a day, but the best time to watch is at sunset. There's a neat little bar you can sit at right on the beach, with a splendid view of the divers. I'll write it down for you." He grabbed a notepad and pen from his shirt pocket and scribbled, "Shrimp Bar."

"Thanks. Where do they learn to do it?"

"These are island boys. They've grown up knowing how. To them, it's natural. They don't fear it at all. It's incredible to watch. You don't want to miss it."

"Thanks for the suggestion. We'll definitely check it out."

After snorkeling, we returned to the villa and napped and read. For both of us, having so much uninterrupted free time, with no obligations, was unusual, and welcomed. Julia was on summer break from teaching 3rd grade and I had left Ramon in charge of my property management responsibilities and current clients. I instructed him to call only if there was a dire emergency. While Julia was out for a stroll, I ordered room service for later, some warm chocolate chip cookies, and a pitcher of cold milk. It would be perfect for after dinner when we returned. We could sit in the jacuzzi and enjoy our favorite snack. I love the fact that warm chocolate chip cookies and cold milk is the favorite of both of us.

We arrived at the little bar just in time for sunset. It was situated right off the beach, and the slate floor was covered with a layer of fine sand. We ordered cold beers and coconut-crusted shrimp and trained our eyes to the top of the cliff. I started feeling very ill. My stomach rolled and flipped, and I feared I would vomit.

"Honey, I don't feel well. I better head to the restroom," I told Julia.

"No, the divers are about to jump. It's sunset. It's almost time. Duncan, you'll miss it. Take a deep breath. You'll be okay. You're probably feeling lightheaded from snorkeling and too much sun." She rested her hand on mine.

"You look a bit pale, though. Can you hang on till we see them?"

I wanted to bolt. The sight of people jumping off a cliff was not a good idea for me. I started flashing back to the night. I had pushed it too far by planning to watch cliff divers on the anniversary of the incident. What had I been thinking?

"Look! They're getting ready."

Everyone in the bar oriented their bodies to face the cliff. I glanced up to see three divers lining up at the cliff's edge and to hear the bartender say, "No way. They're doing a three? They never do that. Look, everyone. This is really amazing. They never do a three-man jump. The last time they did it… nevermind, just watch. And cross your fingers."

I don't think anyone could look away after that. Eyes riveted to the scene, we all watched as the three men took a step forward and, in synchronicity, executed perfect dives. They were so in sync; they appeared as one diver against the rocky cliff face. Collective breath was held until we saw three glistening, wet bodies scrambling up from the water to a ledge, then grabbing hands and taking a bow.

"That was bananas!" the bartender shouted enthusiastically, and everyone cheered, including me. My stomach felt better, and we ordered some giant onion rings, a salad to share, and two more cold beers. When the bartender learned we were newlyweds, he brought us two shots of tequila to celebrate.

"Let's leave the Jeep and just get a cab back to the villa," I suggested.

"Yeah, good idea. We shouldn't drive yet, and I'm getting chilly. I should have brought my jacket."

During the ride, I could feel the beginning of another headache, and not wanting to spoil the evening, I said to Julia, "Go ahead and get in the Jacuzzi. I'll be right out."

I went to the bathroom and splashed cold water on my face, but that seemed to make it worse, and it gave me chills. *I hope I'm not coming down with something. Not now, not on my honeymoon. I cannot get sick.* I switched to hot water, closed my eyes, and breathed in the steam. This was a trick that always seemed to make me feel better, alternating between splashing my face with cool water and hot water. I discovered the remedy by accident during one of my migraine episodes in high school. I splashed the heated water on my face a few times, grabbed a towel, and looked in the mirror. There was something written there. I couldn't quite see it, so I turned the water on with only hot to make more steam. The message on the mirror read, "I know what you did."

I blacked out, apparently hitting my head on the edge of the vanity on my way to the floor. I nicked my scalp, making a minor cut which bled profusely because of the amount of aspirin I'd consumed all day to keep the headache from turning into a migraine. Julia said she heard me groan, then fall and came in to find me on the floor with a lot of blood. She called 911 in a panic. I woke to three paramedics looking over me, checking my pulse. One had waved smelling salts, and that had done the trick for me to regain consciousness. The cut on my head was tiny and would not need stitches, just a bit of glue to hold it together. Was I sure I didn't need to go to the hospital? I insisted I was fine. The paramedics wanted to take me in for a CAT scan but agreed to let Julia monitor me and not let me sleep for a few hours. I was more embarrassed than anything else. After they left, Julia asked what happened, as I knew she would.

"I don't know," I said, "I had a headache and was splashing hot and cold water on my face, then I just felt super dizzy, and I guess I blacked out."

"That's it?"

"Yeah, it was strange. That's never happened to me."

"Here, let me clean you up."

She turned the tap and let the hot water run, and steam filled the bathroom again. *Now she is going to see the message*, I thought, *How will I explain it? How will I explain my reaction?* I stood up and grabbed a towel, intending to wipe it off. Another spell of dizziness threatened. I grabbed the counter. We both looked at the mirror, and there it was. "I know what you did," clearly written in the steam.

Julia said, "Oh, there's my message. I wrote it earlier. Did you see it?" Then the doorbell rang.

"Hold on, I'll get it. I know what it is." Julia hurried to answer the door.

I sat down on the toilet lid and cradled my head in my hands. I did not know what to do or think. Julia came back in with a tray. The chocolate chip cookies and cold milk had arrived. I'd forgotten I ordered them.

"Here, have one," Julia said, offering a warm cookie wrapped in a napkin. "Let's go sit on the lanai."

"Sure," I said and followed her out of the bathroom, still a little shaky on my feet.

"It was so funny when I called room service to order cookies and milk. They asked if I wanted a double order. I said, 'Um, no.' Then I figured out you had the same idea. Isn't that funny?"

"So is that what the message was?"

"Yes. Great minds think alike Duncan. I already knew we were perfect for each other, but somehow the cookie order really nailed it for me."

2010

THE BULLDOZERS, GRADERS, AND construction trucks inched up the mountain with the purpose of widening the road and installing more guard rail. People complain the roads are unsafe and too narrow. Cyclists insist on using them and every time I see one, I shudder, thinking they are taking their life in their hands, especially on the blind turns. Residents have been divided on the issue for years. Some are in favor of widening the road to increase safety for cyclists and walkers. Others wish to leave it alone, repair the potholes as needed, nothing more, fearing if they widen the road, it will only encourage more visitors to the area, more outsiders using the trails. They want to keep it effectively closed except to residents. I've felt edgy with all the commotion happening near "the spot," so I've been avoiding the route that would take me past it. The ravine is so overgrown that at this point I wonder if there would be any evidence of the night or if it would have long been destroyed.

I checked out a couple of properties in the lower village and met with a client looking to lease his office building. When

I arrived at the office, it was after 1 pm. I found my office mates gathered around the TV in the lobby and I could see that the Channel 3 news reporter was on.

Must be a local interest story. "What's up?" I asked casually.

"They just uncovered a body when they were grading the hill to widen the road, up on Ocean View. Watch, they're talking about it now."

I crowded in and saw our local reporter standing by the twisty tree right near the place.

Deep breaths.

"Yes, folks, so we're just learning that the crew doing the grading has uncovered what appears to be the remains of a person down in this ravine off Ocean View Drive. We have no details yet, but police and the coroner are on the way and we'll keep you informed as we learn more."

The camera switched to a long shot that looked like it was from the vantage point of a helicopter or drone. Below, I could see a mound covered with a blue tarp on the shoulder of the road. I stiffened but tried to act natural. Everyone seemed to have a comment. I listened but did not contribute to the conversation.

"That is a body, no doubt."

"Ugh, they just keep playing this clip over and over."

"I don't think we're going to learn anything else today. They'll have to call in a forensic specialist."

"I wonder whose body it is. Did they say if it's an adult or a child? So creepy. It's gotta be foul play, right?"

"Are there any local missing person cases?"

"I wonder if there's a murderer on the loose?"

"Maybe a serial killer."

"Don't say that! That would tank our property values."

"Hey Knight, you look so pale. What's up?"

"Yeah, this kind of stuff just freaks me out, is all. I just hope it doesn't affect our sales in that area. There are a lot of things I have to do. If you'll excuse me. I'm gonna get back to work."

And with that, I retreated to my office, imaging sets of eyes following me. I closed the door and the mini blinds. Just breathe, I told myself. If this is it, you've had your years of freedom, fifteen years. Even if it is a body, which I felt certain it was, there's really no mistaking human remains. It means nothing. Nothing has changed for me, I reasoned. I pushed the thought out of my mind and poured myself into work. Hours later, the urge to use the bathroom forced me to stand up. I stretched my back, twisting to pop as many vertebrae as I could. I took a cautious peek through the blinds. The office was quiet; the secretary was gone. Good. I preferred not to revisit the earlier conversation.

I left at 5:50 when the coast was clear. Construction on the road had ceased for the day, and the choppers and news vans had taken off. Still, I avoided taking Ocean View from the direction that would pass the construction site. And now "crime scene?" I wondered. I just wanted to get home and allow myself to forget about it. I eased into the driveway, looking forward to dinner and a glass of wine. I hadn't eaten since morning. I kicked off my shoes and left them on the shelf by the front door. I wanted to relax.

"Is that homemade bread I smell?" My spirits lifted.

"Yes, dear. Perfect timing. Come sit down to dinner. We waited for you," Mom said.

Julia sat on the sofa, legs crossed, surrounded by stacks of her students' work. Soft music was playing from the music channel on the TV. Good. The news wasn't on. A cat settled on the back of the sofa behind Julia's head, and Hank stretched out under the coffee table with not a care in the world. Oh, to be a pet.

"Honey, dinner's ready. Duncan's home," Mom called out to Dad.

Dad joined us from his library and we all sat down to eat. Dinner together was a comfortable ritual I appreciated. Being in the safe space of my home, around the people and pets I love, was already making me feel less edgy about the morning's discovery on Ocean View Road. I did not plan to bring up the topic and prayed no one else had seen the news.

"What's this?" I asked Julia, picking up an envelope from my place at the table.

"Oh, I pulled that out of the mailbox this afternoon. It looks like someone hand-delivered it, probably one of your admirers." She smiled. It wasn't unusual for clients to leave gifts, thank-you notes, fresh flowers, or baskets of muffins or fruit their gardener had picked, and many knew where I lived. It's a relatively small town.

Duncan Knight was written in blue ink across the front of the standard white business envelope. It was sealed but had no written address or return address. It reminded me of a note sent home from the teacher to my parents. I couldn't remember any note from a teacher as ever being a good thing. I stuffed it in my pocket without opening it.

"Excuse me." I stood up and headed for the bathroom. "Forgot to wash my hands."

Of course, Hank nudged his way in and stretched out on the bathroom rug at my feet. I reached down to rub his head. I sat on the toilet lid and carefully opened the envelope. I unfolded the lined notebook paper and read the message written in the same blue ink as my name on the envelope.

"*Did you see the news? Are you nervous? You should be. I*

124

know what you did."

No signature. I stuffed the letter back in the envelope and put it in my pocket. I washed my hands and rejoined my family. I acted normal, asking about everyone's day and mentioning the lease for the office building of my client. I laughed along with my parents as Julia described some antics of her students, but I was deeply distracted.

"So, are you going to open the letter?" Julia asked after dinner.

"Oh, I looked at it when I went to the bathroom. You were right," I lied. "It was a thank you from a client, a gift card for Village Coffee. All my clients seem to know it's my favorite."

"OOOh, nice. I think I just used my last one from my students."

Julia is always getting gift cards for Village Coffee and we have a little competition of who gets more. I needed to leave so I could think in private. I pretended to check my email on my phone after dinner.

"Honey, I'm sorry I've got to go back to the office. There's some paperwork I need to finish. A selling agent just countered an offer. It might be a while. Don't wait up." I hated lying, but I couldn't think of an alternative. It was the easiest way.

I parked in the lot behind Village Real Estate and entered through the back door. It was dark. The yellow street lamp cast a light glow by the back entrance. The motion sensor lights came on as I walked in. No one was in the office. Everyone had left much earlier for the day, and there was no paperwork that I needed to catch up on. Still, I went into my office and closed the door. I turned on my desktop computer, pulled up the news, and re-watched the footage from earlier. There was nothing new. Next, I searched for a forensics website. I wanted to figure out how investigators would tell the age of the remains that were recovered. I found a forensic anthropology website and learned that a trained professional could determine many things from recovered bones, including whether they are human, the approximate age and sex of the person, and often the cause of death, which can lead to a criminal investigation. This was not comforting.

My thoughts went back to the note. What was that about? And who would put it in our personal mailbox? There was no one who witnessed that night. How could there be? Someone is just wanting to mess with me. Probably the same kids who write "Killer" on my ads. Or maybe it's a disgruntled client. There have been a few who blamed me for not getting the deal they wanted. I admit, I've been called gruff and other not-too-favorable adjectives in several online reviews. Still, I have no shortage of clients. Gruff or not, everyone knows I'm the best at what I do. I can pick who I want to represent, and sorry if you think it's somehow my fault that you can't afford to live in Ocean View Village. Maybe someone felt slighted. That must be it. Has to be.

Two weeks later, I learned the recovered bones were of a female, 5'5 inches tall, approximately 50 years old, Caucasian. There were signs of blunt force trauma. My mind flashed to a scene of a car hitting a person on a dark night, and their body being thrown down the embankment. Blunt force for sure. The scientific expert estimated the skeletal remains to be approximately 20-25 years old, as determined by postmortem decomposition. As far as who the person/victim was, there currently are no leads or links to cold case missing person investigations. Police requested, for anyone who may know the identity of the person, to contact them using the tip line.

I will not be doing that. Twenty to twenty-five years is not fifteen years. But what about that note?

2011

I WASN'T READY FOR Hank to die. I guess no one is when they love their pet like a family member. As the years tick by, you just take for granted that they are there. They don't judge. When Hank slowed down, it was subtle. I didn't notice at first. Our hikes became shorter, then they were more like walks, then strolls, then relaxing in the yard in a patch of sun and just being content to rest. The first time Hank collapsed, I cried. I seldom cry, but the thought overwhelmed me that there would be an end to our relationship. Hank was the only one who really knew me, even better than Julia in some ways. To him I'd confessed all, and he didn't judge, just stared with his deep, soulful, brown eyes as he pushed his weight into me.

Every morning and every evening I mashed his pills into a ball of cheese and even though he hated to take them, he resigned as if he knew it was best. The pills cost $127 per month, which I gladly paid. I would never spend that on myself, but for Hank, anything. Julia was as distraught as I. She loved him. He accepted her cats with a mixture of love and tolerance. At first, the felines were aloof and did not treat him kindly. They'd never lived with a dog before. But their attitudes changed when he chased a hissing possum away from them on our patio, thus proving his loyalty and worthiness. And in his last days, they dutifully kept watch over him, taking turns curling up next to him in his bed, one of the three a constant companion. When he passed on, they mourned and moped and did not eat for two days.

I buried Hank myself in the backyard under the Willow tree and marked the place with a memorial stone that said, "Rest in Peace Hank, the Best Boy." Julia and my parents cried as much as I did and we all reminisced about what a special dog Hank was. After a week, I stopped in at the animal rescue shelter. I'd seen a notice that they were looking for volunteers and I thought I might feel better if I could walk some dogs. The place was depressing. I hated the idea of dogs without loving homes. I'd only entered once before when I found Hank to register him as a "found" and to check if anyone else had registered him as a "lost." After the 14-day period ended, the shelter called to say he was mine if I wanted him because no one had claimed him.

But since that time, I have sent generous donations every year.

When I entered the building, Cindy greeted me. She had on a royal blue staff shirt with a name tag and black shorts and was holding a stack of stainless steel bowls.

"Hi Sir, how can I help you today?"

"I've come to look into volunteering. I just lost my dog…" I paused and took a breath and was surprised to find tears stinging my eyes. "Sorry, just a minute." I turned away. She set the bowls on the counter, came right over, and gave me a quick hug. Normally, I'd flinch, but not today. I needed it.

"I know how hard that is. I'm so sorry." She paused.

"I'm Cindy, I've been here 13 years, and I still get emotional every day whether it's a pet going to a new home, a joyous occasion for sure, or someone surrendering a pet, or what happened yesterday."

"My name is Duncan, Knight actually. Everyone just calls me Knight. What happened yesterday?" I asked, unsure if I wanted to know. I wasn't used to getting emotional at all, but especially not around a stranger. Julia was the one I wanted to have with me. Cindy continued.

"Oh, you're that Knight. I've seen your ads and pictures. Sorry they call you 'Killer', that's not cool at all. Anyway, I don't mean to babble, but thank you. You are one of our best regular donors and we truly appreciate your generosity."

"You're welcome, but could you tell me what happened yesterday?"

"Yes, sorry, I get side-tracked a lot, and I like to talk. Just ask the animals. So, some of our staff went out on a call with the police and Animal Control officers. There were reports of a house with a lot of dogs. It was an unlicensed breeder, and they confiscated all their dogs, lots of puppies. We're forming a waiting list of adopters, but you can certainly have a look. They won't be ready until they've had all their shots and have been spayed or neutered."

"What happened to the parents of the puppies?" I asked.

"They're here too. There are just four that will hopefully be adoptable. I'm sad to say some of the older dogs had to be put down because the conditions were so bad when we got to them. It was the only humane thing to do."

"I want those four dogs," I heard myself say.

"Sir, that's really nice of you, but you don't even know the breeds and haven't met them yet. Honestly, they are in terrible shape and will need a thorough medical work-up before we can even consider permanent homes. But I can show you some other adoptable dogs."

"I lost my dog last week. I'm a great owner and I feel I need to adopt *these* dogs. Does that make sense?" I wasn't even sure it made sense to me.

"Yes, as a matter of fact, it does. Perfect sense. But I don't want you to make a rash decision. These guys have been through a lot and they might fear you or even act aggressive; we haven't evaluated them properly."

"Well, I'd like to see them, and we'll take it from there. You can come and check out my property and decide if I'll be the right fit. I can start as a medical foster. You do that right? I can take the dogs out of the shelter at least temporarily so they can not be so stressed out." I knew I had to be convincing. I was certain that this was what I needed to do.

"Let me meet the dogs, then you'll decide."

"Ok, but it's pretty upsetting. I wasn't directly involved in the rescue, but I was here for the intake. We stayed late into the night, bathing and comforting the dogs. It was a mess. So heartbreaking the conditions they were living in. I'm pretty sure the puppies will be ok because they're so young. They'll be able to bond with people, but the older dogs? It's hard to tell. We really don't know how much human contact they had. The females were in pens and continuously bred, and they tied the males to ropes in the yard. Everything was filthy. Sometimes I hate humans. I'm sorry. I shouldn't say that."

She led me into the back of the shelter where the kennels are located. In one, there were two dogs huddled together.

"These are the two females. We think one is a purebred standard black poodle."

"And the other? She looks like she might be a golden

retriever."

"Yes, that's what we think. The males are a lab and a poodle too. These backyard breeders were trying to produce goldendoodles and labradoodles in various colors and sizes to sell and ship them. They, of course, got greedy and had no clue how to care for dogs. Finally, the neighbors reported them. Thank God."

"Do you mind if I go into the kennel with them?" Something about the way I said it, or the look in my eyes, convinced her.

"Sure, go ahead," she said, adding, "Please be careful."

I undid the latch and slowly crawled into the kennel. The sweet girls were huddled together on a raised dog bed and both flinched as I slowly approached. They had been bathed and given a basic clipping. I could see pink patches on the skin where there must have been matted fur that had to be cut away.

"You poor babies." I cooed in a soft voice, "I'll just sit with you. Would that be ok?" After ten minutes, the black poodle low-crawled over to me. I patiently waited, then set my hand lightly on her head. Her body relaxed, and she gazed up at me with sorrowful eyes. I heard a soft thumping and saw the golden's tail moving.

"Come on, girl, I won't hurt you."

When Cindy returned, both dogs were crowded onto my lap and were allowing me to stroke them softly.

"Oh wow," she whispered, "they have let nobody get close. We had to muzzle and sedate them just to get them clean and clipped. It's like you have a magic touch. I'll figure out a way for you to foster them."

When I crawled out of the kennel, they whimpered and pawed at the chain link.

"I'll be back," I said. "I need to meet the boys, and then I'm taking all of you home."

The male dogs were also together in one of the larger kennels. Cindy explained that they, like the females, were a bonded pair and were inseparable. It would only cause them more distress to be separated, and if adoptable, they should go to the same home.

"Be careful," she warned.

"I don't know how they'll be. They were tied with choke chains. That's why all the fur is rubbed off their necks. I doubt they are used to any kind of human touch, and they're not neutered yet. You probably shouldn't go into the kennel. I'm going to finish the dinner prep in the kitchen and I'll be back in a bit."

It appalled me how thin they were. I could see their ribs. The chocolate lab let out a low warning growl and stood in front of the tan poodle as if to protect his friend.

At first, I cried silently and then with a big gasp. The tears flowed at will and I did not hold back. I wrapped my arms around my middle and squatted to the floor. I was overwhelmed with the grief of losing Hank and with the way these dogs had been treated by humans. It was at this moment, Julia came and sat next to me, wrapping her arms around me and laying her head on my shoulder.

"How did you know?"

"I had a feeling you needed me, so here I am. Plus, I called home and Dad said you might come here after work."

This is why Julia is perfect for me. She gets me. After the little growl and the showing of teeth, Mack let his guard down. My crying helped him feel safe. Morty was submissive from the start. He seemed relieved to be with us. As for the girls, we named the Golden Retriever Betsy and the poodle

Moxie.

It took little convincing for Cindy to let us take the dogs the same evening. I thanked her and made another hefty donation for the care of the puppies. We agreed to take "our" dogs to our personal veterinarian right away and promised to be responsible to spay and neuter them. I waited for the dogs to eat their dinners while Julia filled out the paperwork.

"Should we call Mom and Dad and give them a heads-up that we're bringing home four dogs?" Julia asked.

"Sure, you can call, but I have a feeling they won't be surprised. I told them I was visiting the rescue today to volunteer. Dad said it's been too quiet without Hank lately."

"Let's call. I'll put them on speaker."

As always, my parents were supportive. They were excited to meet the dogs.

"I'll get some old comforters ready; we can get proper beds for them tomorrow," Mom said.

"I'm going to gather Hank's toys. I think we still have treats in the pantry. This is going to be fun. Four dogs. Duncan, you never cease to surprise us! Come home soon, I want to meet these dogs," Dad sounded like an excited kid.

Now it was Julia's turn for tears.

"I love you two so much. How did I get this lucky?" She gushed to Mom and Dad.

"Oh Honey! We love you too. We love you both," Mom laughed, "now bring home those dogs!"

Cindy gave us four leashes and collars and helped us get the dogs into our two cars.

"Don't expect too much of them. They'll need lots of time and patience to decompress. Call my cell if you have any concerns at all. Are you sure you're okay with taking them?"

"Yes. Don't worry, we've got this. I promise."

Cindy planned to visit the next day. Normally, this would happen before the adoption, but we were breaking all kinds of rules this evening.

The four new arrivals made themselves at home faster than any of us expected. We kept them contained in the main living room area. They sniffed around and came right up to my parents, allowing them to feed them treats and pet them.

"They can feel our energy," Julia said, "and they know they're safe."

"I'm staying on the couch tonight," Dad said. "I don't want them getting nervous in the middle of the night."

"Dad, you don't need to do that. I can stay out here."

"No, it's no trouble," his voice betrayed him. I could hear the emotion. "I've missed Hank so much. I'm glad you saved these guys. The cats have been really lonely."

We didn't know how the cats would react or if the dogs were familiar with cats at all. We had our answer the next morning when the four dogs and three cats all gathered in the kitchen for breakfast. It seemed they were fine with each other. Cindy arrived mid-morning to check on us and was impressed with the property and with how seamlessly all four dogs were adjusting to our family.

"If you would ever consider being official fosters, let me know. This is a magnificent piece of land with plenty of room. We could fence in a sizable area for the dogs... Sorry, I was just thinking out loud. I do that sometimes. Bad habit. But if you ever wanted to foster, the shelter would cover the expenses and provide the volunteers. Often dogs do better in a home environment when we try to find them new families. They're so much less stressed when they're not cooped up in a kennel."

"Well, that's something we might consider," Mom said. I

wasn't sure if she was just being polite.

"In any case, we need to let these four settle in, and we'll get back to you," I said.

"Do you think you might want to keep more than one of these dogs?" Cindy sounded hopeful.

"We definitely want to keep all four. No question," Julia said, and my parents and I nodded in agreement. It was the perfect way to honor Hank, to give these four a second chance.

"They are so lucky," Cindy gushed. "Keep in touch and let us know how they're doing and if you need anything. You've made my day!"

"Absolutely, will do," I replied, smiling.

Our "family" of seven was now a family of eleven, and we were well pleased.

Later, I walked over to the willow tree where we buried Hank. I often sit and chat with him. Someone had left wildflowers next to his memorial stone. *How sweet*, I thought. When I mentioned it, neither my parents nor Julia had done it.

"Maybe the housekeepers or the pool man. Everyone loved Hank," Mom said and didn't seem phased.

"Yes, that's probably it," I agreed. But I felt unable to square the uneasy feeling in my gut, as if someone had intruded in my private space.

2012

J UST THROW IT OUT, they'll never know the difference. This is the advice people gave me since the first time a notice to appear for Jury Duty came in the mail. It was tempting. Over the years I've shown up, spent the day waiting in an uncomfortable chair, wondering if I'll get picked and hoping I won't. I thought about postponing it, but there was no good excuse not to go and by the time the date rolled around, it was too late for a postponement. I walked through the metal detector and set it off with my keys. I put my keys in the tray, along with my phone, walked through the archway a second time, and was passed over with an additional metal detecting wand. Then I followed the signs to room 240. I turned in my notice, collected my name badge with my group number, slid it into the laminate sleeve, clipped it to my shirt, and took a seat as far away from others as possible. I put on my headphones and balanced my laptop on my thighs. May as well do some work and catch up on some podcasts.

By noon, it was time for lunch and my group number had

not yet been called. If I could make it till three, I'd be in the clear, my civic duty complete for the year. During the lunch break, I walked around the government center and found a labyrinth. I zoned out, walking it and before I knew it; it was time to go back in. I'd taken up all the time from the break and had never eaten lunch. The protein bar in my jacket pocket would have to suffice. But, after the break, my number was called, and I followed the group, feeling like a cow being herded into a pen. This would be a multi-week trial, and it was made clear that they would excuse only a few people.

One by one, potential jurors raised their hands and stated their case of why they should be sent home. I had no good reason and figured it's my civic duty, I may as well serve. If necessary, my job was flexible enough to rearrange appointments and I could work non-traditional hours.

Others in the room had kids (why hadn't they used this excuse not to be here in the first place), they owned a business that no one else could run, they had medical issues of one kind or another, and on and on. I racked my brain for a viable excuse and could think of none, so I sat and listened to the myriad of creative reasons the other potential jurors gave. I made it through the first round and was asked to come back for day two. The lawyers were narrowing the field.

As I left the building, I saw a man in an orange jumpsuit being led past me and into a van from the city jail. He gestured wildly and shouted, "Hey, what the hell are you looking at? I know what you did."

"What?" I shouted back, knowing it was unwise to engage, but unable to help myself after a long, frustrating day, plus the guy was in shackles. It wasn't as if he could harm me.

"You know me," he snarled back. The police officer told

him to knock it off and get in the van. It was jarring. I put my head down and walked with long strides to my car as quickly as possible. I sat for a minute, taking deep belly breaths to calm down. I hate confrontation, especially with a random insane person. Why would he say that? Why to me? I wished I had thrown the jury duty notice in the trash.

The next day, I showed up again. This is where the questions got more specific and I think we all suspected we were being considered as jurors for the robbery and assault at the elementary school that had occurred downtown a few months earlier. So how could I put across that I might be biased in my deliberation of a case like this? After all, my wife is a teacher. I would want the suspect to pay for what he'd done. Turns out I didn't have to. The defendant's court-appointed attorney excused me. So I guess I get another year jury duty free.

Still, something about the case was bothering me. I could not be certain if the trial was for the crime I'd read about in the newspaper, but I wanted to know more. Of course, I turned to Mom, the best sleuth I know, for help.

"It was Lincoln Elementary," she said. "That's where it happened. I've always thought it was dangerous how the classroom doors open right out onto the street at that school. I've always thought someone could just walk right up, and sure enough."

"Well, what happened exactly? What did you find out, Mom?"

"Here, I'll read it to you." Mom opened her laptop to the tab she had saved with the report and read aloud the important parts.

"During the middle of the school day at Lincoln Elementary, a homeless man entered the art room and approached the teacher. He brandished a pocket knife and demanded she give him her purse, which she did. He then asked her to unlock a cabinet and give him spray paint. When she told him she had no spray paint, he shoved her to the floor and attempted to flee, pushing over a desk and hurting a child, age 10, who suffered minor injuries. A quick-thinking student ran out to get help during the altercation, and as the suspect tried to leave the scene, two other staff members from the school apprehended him."

"That's pretty intense for those kids. How scary," I said. "Is there a picture of the guy?"

"Yes, look. Here, I'll make it bigger. Let me zoom in."

I leaned down by my mom to view the mug shot. It was a blurry photo of a dirty and disheveled man with matted brown hair, a thin mustache, and a disturbed snarl on his face. The name said, "David Miller." He had crazy, haunted eyes. He looked like every other homeless man I'd ever seen. Rumpled, wild-eyed, anonymous. I glanced away, disgusted, unable to tell if it was the same person who'd yelled at me as I left the courthouse. But I was definitely sure I didn't know this man, or the one who shouted at me, whether or not they were the same person.

"I'm going to pray for that poor soul," Mom said. "He looks like he could use it."

"True," I replied, "But maybe we should pray for the teacher and the kids he frightened."

Mom can be too compassionate sometimes.

When the trial was over, the man got six months in jail and community service. He was not to come within 25 feet of any school as part of the agreement. They awarded no damages to the teacher involved, probably because the criminal was a drifter and wouldn't be able to pay anything, anyway. I couldn't help but envision someone walking into Julia's classroom and threatening her. The idea filled me with rage, and I have no doubt I could easily injure or kill anyone who threatened her. Part of me wants her to quit her job and stay home or work with me at my office. There is plenty she could do to keep busy and we certainly don't need the money she makes. I have enough sense not to ask this of her, so I keep my mouth shut, and never let on how I worry about her whenever she isn't with me. I only want to protect her. The parents of the injured child planned to sue the school. The teacher would continue in her current job. This did not surprise me.

2013

J ULIA AND I SAT near the shore on a plaid blanket. We leaned in to warm our hands over the small fire we'd built. Technically, fires aren't allowed, but it's an unspoken rule of the locals to turn a blind eye. So, often people will make a little fire in the protected cove. Dogs are forbidden too, as stated on large signs posted at the top and bottom of the trail, a rule also not adhered to by locals, including us. This evening we had our four dogs along and one of the fosters. They were splashing and running in the surf, digging and rolling in the sand, and dragging long ropes of kelp around. The timid little foster dog, a terrier type we were calling "Toto,"was learning how to play.

"He's going to make a wonderful pet for the lucky family who adopts him," Julia said. "I love how our pack acts like ambassadors for all our new guys. It's pretty amazing to watch." Our pack includes Betsy, Moxie, Mack and Morty, our original four rescue dogs.

After taking on the four, Cindy successfully convinced us to become fosters in conjunction with the animal shelter, and after a temporary trial, we decided we loved it. The pool house makes a perfect office for volunteers and has space to store supplies. Students from the local high school need community service hours and working with our foster dogs is fast becoming a popular way to earn those hours. Volunteers get to play with and socialize the dogs to get them ready for their future home placements. We installed extra fencing to create two large yards and one small yard for our family and foster dogs. We are up to keeping ten dogs at a time and helping to place them with the best fit adopters for each dog's temperament and personality. Mom has a special knack for this and she's enjoying updating the adoption page and blogging about each dog we foster. She has them photographed in funny outfits or with silly props and describes them as if they are on a dating site, carefully playing up their good qualities while downplaying any challenging behaviors. It's hard not to want to keep them all, but the more we find new homes for, the more we can save. I never pass up the opportunity to mention I foster dogs when I sell a property. As a result, many are placed locally.

Julia packed our favorite wine and some cheese and crackers. We were in time to watch the sunset. It was beautiful, streaking the sky with shades of pink, red, and purple, then slowly fading out to dusk. We were about ready to pack up and gather the beasts when they all started barking at once.

"Quiet down guys! You're disturbing the peace!" The dogs were gathered by the shore and were looking at something. Morty, the tan poodle, ran over and barked, then ran back to the shore.

"I think he wants us to check something out," Julia said.

"I'll go," I volunteered, and stood to walk over to see what all the commotion was about.

And then I saw it.

"Hey Jules, there's a tiny boat in the cove. Come look." The boat was a small metal rowboat about 35 feet from the shore. At first, it was hard to make out if anyone was in it. It appeared empty, abandoned. Julia met me at the shoreline. The dogs continued to bark, and Betsy and Mack started to swim out in the surf.

"Maybe it came loose from a dock in the harbor and floated over. Do you think I should try to grab it?" I was barefoot and could ditch my pants and shirt and swim the short distance in my underwear.

"Hey, I think there's a person in the boat," Julia shouted, pointing.

"Is someone there? Do you need help?" I could make out the shape of a person as the boat bobbed up and down in the waves, and I didn't think we should wait for a response.

"I'm gonna swim out. Call 911."

I stripped down to my boxers and waded in. The water was icy, much colder than I expected. The surf was mellow in the cove and it was an easy swim for me, flanked on either side by Betsy and Mack, the two retrievers. I reached the boat and grabbed the side, pulling myself up to peer in. Curled up on the floor of the boat next to the bench seat was a man wrapped up in a rubber rain slicker. Even though it was getting dark, I knew it was yellow. I panicked as I do every time I see a similar jacket and am mentally transported to the night of the incident, accident, crash, whatever it was. I reached in and grabbed part of the jacket, asking, "Sir, are you ok?"

"Necesito ayuda," came the reply. I saw a rope connected near the front of the boat that must have been used to tie it to a dock. I grabbed the rope and swam back to shore while towing the boat behind me. There was no point in getting into the boat. I saw no oars. Once I could stand close to shore, I moved behind the boat and I pushed it in. Minutes later, we heard the sirens up on the bluff. Help had arrived.

"Can you stand?" I asked the man. Then I switched to my rudimentary Spanish and tried, "Se puede levantar?"

"Si, Si," he replied, and stood on shaky legs. "Estoy perdido, estoy perdido."

"He's saying he's lost." Julia understood him better than I. "What is your name? Nombre?" I asked.

"Jorge," he replied.

We helped him out of the boat and walked him over to our blanket. The fire had died down and was almost out. I handed him a bottle of water from our pack and pulled out the battery lantern, and switched it on. There was still some light left, but darkness was setting in. Two paramedics came down the trail, followed by a sheriff whom I recognized in the lantern light as Sheriff Shiloh. Julia quickly explained what happened and that the man's name was Jorge and he was lost. The paramedics were checking out Jorge and asking questions in Spanish. Sheriff Shiloh told us the man's family had reported him missing earlier that afternoon when the daughter had come home from work and he wasn't there. Their home is in the harbor. Jorge's daughter panicked when she also noticed the rowboat was gone and family members feared the worst. Apparently Jorge had been talking about taking out the boat, but had done so telling no one and with no supplies.

"It's lucky you found him when you did or this may not have ended well," the Sheriff said. "The daughter said he never learned to swim and takes medications."

"I'm glad I could help," I replied, and I truly was.

"Please make sure that fire, which I will pretend I didn't see, is put out completely before you leave."

"Will do."

"Do all these dogs belong to you as well?"

"Four of them do and one's a foster. We foster dogs for the animal shelter. We've met before. My name's Duncan Knight. I'm a realtor, and this is my wife, Julia."

"I remember, yes. As a matter of fact, we just lost our family pet and my girls are devastated. Maybe you could help us find a new family dog."

"We would love to," Julia said. "Duncan, give him your card." I dug one out of my wallet and handed it to him.

"Call my cell or office line any time."

"I will, and thank you again. You did a good deed here tonight. You probably saved that man's life." He walked away, then turned back, saying, "Are you still interested in the local crime scene?"

"Sure. I like to keep up with anything of concern, but my wife's the one who's a big fan of crime shows."

"That's right," Julia said. "I never miss an episode of True Crime."

"D'ya hear about the remains we uncovered?" The Sheriff asked.

"You mean from a couple of years ago?" I replied.

"Yup, cold case. No leads. It's our own local unsolved mystery."

"That's interesting," I choked out. "Have a good evening Sheriff."

The next day, a giant basket arrived at the office filled with all kinds of culinary delights from the family of Jorge along with a card expressing their heartfelt thanks. A reporter came to take my photo for a write-up in the Village Reporter.

I wasn't used to the attention and did not welcome it, but realized the notoriety might be good free advertising. **Local Realtor, Duncan Knight and Wife Julia Make Daring Ocean Rescue.** Definitely good for business.

Then, two days later, a letter arrived. Addressed to me at my office location, a standard white business envelope with my name written on the front in blue ink, but with no stamp.

Exactly like the one left in my home mailbox a few years ago. Someone had slipped it into the regular stack of mail. Inside was a clipping of the news article with *Fraud* written on it in black marker and a sheet of notebook paper. Scrawled on the paper, *I still know what you did. Killer.* Unsigned. This time I did not save it. I tore it into pieces and put the pieces in the shredder. Then I went into Ramon's office and asked him to pour me a scotch.

"What are we celebrating?" he asked, happy to oblige and pour himself one as well.

"Nevermind," I said, taking a hefty gulp and plopping onto his sofa.

2014

THE FIRES LAST DECEMBER were devastating. Conditions were perfect following a drought that had dragged on for ten years with no end in sight. Conserving water was the new norm.

Everyone was expected to replace their grass yards with turf or decomposed granite and succulents meant to grow in a desert with little or no water. Some neighborhoods looked more like Arizona than California. You didn't dare hose down your driveway or attempt to wash your car if the neighbors could see. You'd only get looks of reproach and maybe even reported and fined. Of course, you could take your vehicle to the car wash, your only option really, and get soaked for $25 just to drive through.

In our hills, it is mandated that property owners thin the brush and create a buffer zone of at least 100 feet around their homes and any outbuildings. As a kid I enjoyed this job until one day when I was powering the weed whacker, feeling like a superhero taking out four foot tall bushes and grass swishing the blade back and forth. It was so satisfying until I passed that blade over an innocent mouse family living in the brush. I was devastated and inconsolable. My mom assured me it wasn't my fault. An accident, circle of life and all that, but I never picked up the weed whacker again. All the fun had been sucked out of it and replaced with the guilt of killing an innocent family. Ever since, we paid professional gardeners to cut back the brush, and I made it my business to learn enough Spanish to persuade them to be careful of mice, bunnies and any other living creatures. They just nodded with a dead-eye stare at the privileged little boy.

New construction, which is fairly rare, is now built with an automatic sprinkler system on the inside and out. So a bag of burnt popcorn can literally ruin an entire section of your house with flooding if you're not careful. Gone too are wood-burning fireplaces, replaced with gas insert models that "burn" artificial logs.

On the day the fires started, the winds had been whipping for the better part of a week. I arrived home early, 4:30, to find the power out. It was getting dark, and I wondered where I could gather the needed supplies. We had lanterns and candles, but nothing was organized.

Organizing emergency supplies, except for the rescues, was always put off. I needed to call all the dogs in; the wind was blowing ferociously, and I didn't want to risk anyone getting spooked and taking off. It was a hot dry wind, unusual for December, but those were the Santa Anas. Hot, dry and unsettling. If I hadn't gone into the office and later had to show a home to new clients, I would have worn shorts that day. At the office it was just me and the new secretary. She had the news streaming on her desktop.

"Wow, Mr. Knight, it sure is a windy one."

"Please call me Knight, no Mr." I'd said it a hundred times.

"This just feels scary. I left Kansas to avoid tornadoes and now I feel like I'm stuck in one. It's way too warm for December, too. Never thought I'd say it, but I miss the snow. There is no seasons here."

'*Are,*' I thought, but refrained from correcting her. I'd been accused in the past of being "gruff," and "intimidating and unapproachable" so I was trying not to be.

While that was true about having no real distinguishable seasons, it got old hearing non-Californians bark about it. As far as I'm concerned, they can have their snow. It's pretty and pristine for a day, then it just looks miserable and dirty and you're stuck inside with layers of clothing, and everybody's fat. I know I sound like an awful person, but that's how I feel and I'm entitled to my opinions. The fire gauge on the station across the street showed red, extreme fire danger, and had for months. She kept talking.

"I'm feeling homesick. I really am."

Go back. I thought contemptuously. Then, *Why am I such a jerk?*

Nice enough girl, but the last thing I wanted was to listen to her prattle on. And those nails, the worst. Close to three inches long and pointed like knives, and airbrushed, which I thought was out of style as of the 90s, two-toned red and green for the holiday season. How does Paul, the boyfriend, deal with it? Maybe he likes them as a back scratcher or something. I know there must be others in the office equally appalled as I was but no one dared mention the nails. That would be sexist. When Julia spotted the offending nails while at my office, she had gone on and on about it until I stopped her.

I asked, "What do you want me to do? You're aware I can't say a thing. I'm a man."

"Yeah, I get it. Next time I'm in, maybe I'll casually bring it up by asking if that's how the girls wear their nails in Kansas," she said.

But she never brought it up that I recall, and now we were blessed with the Christmas nail version. I suggested we cut out early. No one was likely to come in during this wind and I'd finished my appointments for the day. The forecast was saying the gusts were 70 to 80 miles an hour. Prime fire conditions. Why do they keep talking about prime conditions when there could be some psycho listening just ready to drop a match for his own personal glory? And just like that, someone who remains unidentified, did. The result, far-reaching and tragic.

When I got in the car, I heard the ping of an alert on my phone again. It was a strong wind warning, with downed trees and power outages possible. Why hadn't I gathered together a proper emergency kit? I turned on the local AM news station for my quick drive up the hill. Even the newscasters seemed flustered.

"We're just getting reports of a fire in Paula Serra."

I felt bad for that town. It certainly had its share. There was a fire there just last year that burned a lot of the quaint little downtown area. It's a mostly rural farming community with generations of ranchers and middle-to-lower-income folks. Good people. It's where Julia teaches 3rd grade.

"We have reports that the fire started in the Citrus Grove neighborhood, near the elementary school."

Holy crap. That's Julia's school. I hope she's on her way home and safe. She is forever staying late to plan lessons, help with clubs, and have meetings, always meetings. School is out at three, but she usually gets home closer to five, after her 20-minute commute. I remembered then how she'd called

154

earlier. Her school was closing early because the winds were deemed dangerous. The campus is located on a two-lane highway and authorities wanted to keep it clear.

Julia arrived home about 30 minutes after me, just as my parents and I were starting to have genuine concern for her safety. I ran out to meet her. The wind whipped furiously, stronger than I'd ever felt, bending and breaking tree branches, and the sound was otherworldly and ominous.

"Here, help me with these supplies," Julia shouted.

She popped her trunk and hefted out a 20-pound bag of dog food and I could see there was more in there. Just like her to think ahead. She pulled out lanterns with fresh batteries as well, and large jugs of water. If the power was out, we'd be fine. We had the generator, but it wouldn't do for the rescues to run out of food. Julia always thought of the animals first. I loved this about her. Knowing the wind made many of the dogs nervous, she'd put the new fosters inside when she was home earlier and left access only through the doggie door to the small and secure side yard. The larger yards, though mostly secure, could be escaped by a scared or determined dog via a breach in the fencing or a swiftly dug tunnel. It had happened once before, resulting in Franny, who was new to the rescue and had not been spayed nor chipped, taking off and being recovered a month later, pregnant with a litter of eight puppies. They were the "Snack Food" puppies, and all found homes swiftly due to the popularity of the rescue webpage. I laugh as I think about how we named them: Cracker Jack, Hot Cheeto, Dorito, Frito, Jolly Rancher, Fiddle, Faddle, and Skittles. The mom was a small black and white terrier mix, and the babies looked like they had eight different fathers. All the chosen adopters keep in touch and post updates and pictures regularly on the shelter webpage.

With all humans and animals safely inside, there was nothing to do but sit tight and wait.

The origin of the fire was just over 20 miles away and it was not likely to travel to where we were. But as the evening wore on, the winds picked up, and the fire was tearing across the mountaintop at an unbelievable speed. We could see the glow in the near distance and feel the heat coupled with the unseasonably warm Santa Ana winds. It was an eerie and helpless feeling. The four of us watched TV in shock, seeing houses consumed in flames. A real-time color-coded map showed evacuation orders continuing to expand, and knowing we had to move 15 dogs, our three ornery and elderly cats, and two older parents if the orders expanded to include us, we grabbed the most important items, and a few essentials. And then the power went out.

Thankfully, three of our trusted volunteers showed up. One took all four small dogs, and the other volunteers took two big dogs each. We'd need to deal with the other seven. There were too many and not enough space for crates. Three had not yet been vetted for friendliness with other canines or humans, but as we loaded them, with only their leashes, into three cars, mine, Julia's, and Dad's, miraculously, they seemed to sense that this was no time for conflict. Just get along and we'll all survive. You can decide later if you like your new roommates. Dogs know.

My parents' medications, dogs, cats, and their food, and a few clothes and personal items for us, and we were off. The only place to go was Dad's office. Mine was too close, being just down the hill and if the fire was coming and we were officially evacuated, it was likely my office location would be too. Dad's office was in the flatlands, closer to the beach, and was, at one time, a family residence. The accounting office of Knight, Sperry and Thomas was the logical place to go. The neighborhood is a mixture of vacation rentals, businesses, regular homes, and some larger properties that are divided into apartments. At Dad's business, the front half has office space for three accountants, including Dad, who is only a figurehead at this point, and rarely goes in to do any actual work. The back half has a large lounge with several sofas, a restroom, and a fully functional kitchen. At least we would be comfortable. And there's the fenced yard Dad put in when I first brought home his "grand dog" Hank so he could come to work with him. There is still a framed picture of Hank on the mantle, God rest his sweet, gentle soul.

We settled in and Mom got comfortable in the recliner with her favorite cat, an old ginger tabby called Lady Marmalade. Lady Marmalade is a rescue whose growth has been stunted by having too many litters beginning when she was only a kitten herself. Julia brought her to live with us, but she really only likes my mom, and now, at 13, just wants to cuddle and nap and not be bothered. The dogs and other two cats curled up on the throw rugs or the sofa, just happy to be with humans. I'm always in awe of rescues. It's as if they know they've been saved and are just so happy with a little human kindness. We usually only have ten dogs at a time, and we were over capacity at 15, but we also have the best reputation and I knew we'd find permanent homes for these dogs soon enough.

Julia put on a pot of coffee and we settled in on the sofas, glad to still have electricity to watch the news, knowing there would be no sleep that night. It was heartbreaking and unbelievable. The entire mountainside was in flames. It looked as if not a single house would be left standing. People were refusing to leave, dying, trying to spray their own homes with water, and then getting overcome by the inferno. Nine people so far. Nine who thought they could beat back flames with only their grit and a garden hose. We watched in helpless wonder as the flames approached Mountain Lane and continued to Ocean View. And I knew. That was it. My childhood home would not survive this.

When the sun came up, I ventured out. People moved around like zombies, and the flames raged on. The forecast called for wind speeds to increase and the plan was for the firefighters to back off and wait it out; no aerial water drops could be attempted at this time. It was too precarious, too unsafe. There could be no effort to control it. So we waited and watched. When I looked up at the hills, through the haze of thick smoke, I saw bright red lava drizzled everywhere like veins, and if I listened, I could actually hear the roar of the flames through the wind. The fire was a beast devouring property and was moving at the mercy of the ever-shifting winds. The boundaries of the evacuation order extended, and we prepared to move again. It felt like the entire town would be demolished.

By early evening, the wind subsided. The view of the hillsides was still obscured by the thick layers of smoke. The flames had ravaged and moved on and were now settled on the very top and backside of the mountain where no humans lived but wildlife thrived, while continuing their steady march northward to threaten the next town. Behind the smoke were pockets of fire, burning down remains of houses. Only first responders were allowed up the mountain. No one yet knew the extent of the damage. Friends hugged each other and small groups gathered, shell-shocked, in familiar cafes who opened their doors offering free coffee and comfort food. Firefighters worked to tamper down hot spots before the wind stirred again, though we all wondered what could be left to burn. My home and my business most likely were destroyed, but I looked at my wife, my parents, and my rescue animals and felt oddly at peace.

"Thank God we're okay," Mom said.

"Now let's figure out what's next. We can stay here at Dad's office for a while. We'll get the land cleared and rebuild or get an apartment, but we'll need to consider the rescues, too. This will save me from going through my stuff. I always was too much of a packrat. Good thing you had all our photos put on digital. This really helps you understand what's important."

She sounded so strong, so sure, but her eyes were moist and betrayed her words. My parents' whole life was wrapped up in that house. It had been through several remodels and even though it was way too big for just them; it was perfect for the four of us and all our cats and dogs. They loved it and would never have chosen to leave. Mom and Julia had recently begun a new project, an all-white kitchen. When we took on the responsibility of becoming fosters, we made the pool house into an office space for the rescue team. The bedroom had been left alone and held donations of beds, crates, leashes, and toys, but the living area had been re-configured with three desks and a large walk-in pantry for other supplies. A huge restaurant size refrigerator replaced my small apartment-sized one. Where would the volunteers work now? We'd need to rent a really enormous property if we were to continue with the rescue. I had to stop myself. I should be grateful to be alive when others were not as fortunate. I was spared.

Three days later, homeowners were allowed back up into

the hills. We figured it was best for all of us to go together. So Mom, Dad, myself, and Julia took one car, leaving the pups and cats at Dad's office. The village was still cordoned off, and it looked as if many of the businesses had survived. I saw Village Realty and was relieved; smoke had discolored it, but it seemed fine. *No way I'll get lucky twice,* I thought. There were still a few hot spots continuing to burn in the hills. We needed to show proof of residence but were waved up by a friendly officer. Besides the homeowners, there were many just wanting to glimpse the damage, looky-loos just hoping for a chance for a photo. As we wound up the now unfamiliar lanes, we took in the full extent of the damage. Everything was not completely leveled as it had appeared from below. No, the fire had chosen what to destroy and what to save, or maybe the wind had chosen, or God. Where one structure was burnt clear to the ground, another, not 10 feet away, was fully intact, no sign of damage at all. It seemed unfair, so arbitrary. I saw no half-burnt homes. It was all or nothing, completely leveled or untouched. The fire had played hopscotch, leaving about half of the homes unscathed, with even the landscaping looking green and perfect. In other areas, the trees looked like piles of pickup sticks. The ground was covered in fine ash that swirled with the slightest movement, sending particulates into the air. Our eyes and nostrils burned. We were advised to wear masks.

Julia was driving. She took the back way to the house, and I braced myself for the turn that always makes my stomach flip. As Mountain Drive turned into Ocean View Drive, the damage looked worse and worse, and then I saw it. There was the tree, perfect and green, facing the road, and burnt to a crisp facing the ravine. Divided in half by the flames. I wondered if it would live or if the damage was too much. Julia did not know about the significance of this place and didn't see me shudder. When she took the turn, I rolled down my window and leaned out, trying to see down into the ravine. Everything had burned completely. Where before it was choked with small trees and shrubs and bushes such that you couldn't see the fire road below, now it was empty and blackened. I was itching to explore it as soon as possible. We continued on Ocean View Lane; it did not look promising. The five estates leading up to ours were gone-only the random chimney remained, along with mangled rebar. Approaching ours, I expected the same. But our house was still standing. The wooden fences had burned. The trees in the circular driveway were burnt, but not completely decimated; they might even live.

"Stop the car," I said hoarsely.

"This is unbelievable."

"A miracle."

"Praise Jesus."

"Does anyone have their keys on them?"

We entered through the front door like guests and slowly made our way through, no one speaking, just marveling. Part of the large back deck was destroyed and the metal flashing around the roof out back was melted, as if the fire came right up and then retreated, changing its mind. We were spared.

A day later, after we had settled back in with our dogs, cats, and supplies. I took the car and went to check out "the place." The gorge was much deeper than I had previously thought. I could see clearly down to the lower road now. It was steep, with boulders jutting out at angles. All of it had been covered in thick brush and trees before. Now the only tree still standing was the one at the edge of the road. It too might die. It was badly burned on the side facing the cliff. At least I didn't have to wonder anymore. It was all laid bare. I took my mini binoculars out of my pocket and scanned the area all the way down. Next, I walked down the familiar fire road and looked up from the bottom. Daring to take out my binoculars again, I focused and trained them up the hillside. **GUILTY** was scratched into the burnt ashes on the side of a flat face of a boulder wedged into the hill, and under the word was **RIP**. Under that, **DK**. I had to focus the lenses and if I wasn't looking carefully, I would have missed it altogether, but there it was. A message.

Again. I looked around nervously and had the distinct feeling of being watched. The writing had to be fresh, but when and how had someone done it? Was **DK** supposed to be Duncan Knight? This was too surreal.

I climbed up the hill and tried to write with my finger in the ashes on a boulder. I only smudged the ash around. I covered my finger with the tail of my t-shirt and spit on it to moisten it. Now I could write in the ash. I wanted to destroy the message, even while I doubted anyone would see it or if they did, they would have no clue of the significance. I made my way up the side of the mountain using rocks and burnt branches as holds, hoping I wouldn't lose my footing and injure myself and praying under my breath that no one would see me. I reached the rock and rubbed out the words easily. Now I had a clean slate to write my own message. Should it be, **Leave Me Alone**? Or, **I'm Sorry**? Or **I'm Innocent!**? Instead, I scrambled back down writing nothing, dusted the ash off my clothes the best I could, and walked back to my car. That message, or whatever it was, was not necessarily meant for me.

2015

W E ALL WELCOMED THE light drizzle three months after the fire. It made the air feel fresh and even cleaned much of the remaining ash off the buildings. There were warnings. After a fire of that magnitude, the hillsides could be vulnerable to mudslides for years to come with no vegetation to anchor the soil. We knew, but what could anybody actually do about it? The hills needed time to repair themselves, for fresh brush to grow, for trees to be planted. Everything and everyone needed a chance to heal. The rain was like a blessing, a cleansing, a fresh start, and as long as it was light, we should be okay. Further down the coast, ten years before, a small beach town whose front yard is the ocean and backyard is a huge mountain, got 5 inches of rain in an hour after two weeks of on-again off-again storms. It proved too much and with no warning at all, the mountain slid into the town and seven of the 30 homes were covered. In one family, only an older sister survived. Her parents and three younger siblings were buried in the mud. The remaining properties were valued at zero, and the residents were ordered to leave. But the die-hard townspeople wouldn't leave their homes. On the top of the slide area, five crosses were erected in a makeshift memorial. For years afterward, every time it rained at all, the people of the town would temporarily leave. Eventually, the property values rebounded, and the remaining residents forgot the devastating trauma.

So the possibility of a mudslide loomed in the back of the minds of the people. Owners were finally having their properties cleared of the hazardous waste produced by the fire and were seeking the proper permits to rebuild. I had a heck of a time scrambling to secure rentals for my clients who had lost homes. Any available properties below the hillsides were selling over the asking price, with multiple offers and rentals going to the highest bidders. Places that no one was interested in before became coveted as inventory was low and owners who lost homes scrambled to hire architects and contractors, wanting to rebuild bigger and better than before. Jane's parents' old house had burned. Jane called and asked me about it, and she cried when I confirmed it was a total loss.

"I spent my whole childhood there," she said.

I understood. I went over to the site of the home and walked out onto the foundation remembering the times I'd spent there with my friends during our middle school and high school years. Then I reflected on the party and on the pivotal night where I'd unwisely left, and all the turmoil that one decision managed to cause. I felt sorry for the family I'd sold the house to and I helped them find a rental near the beach while they decided on a plan. Every time I was asked if my home burned too, when I replied, "No, I was lucky," I felt guilty.

The drizzle turned to rain; the rain turned to a downpour, and during the early morning hour of 4 am on a Sunday, the mountain came down. Storm drains were clogged. The water, mud, and debris, with nothing to hold them back, diverted to other paths and took out ten homes on their journey down the mountain and through the village, stopping only at the ocean's edge where it mixed with the sea in ugly brown waves. Once again, my house was spared from the path of destruction, as was my office. Why? I will never know.

It seemed only fair that Julia and I volunteered to help clear the mud to recover possessions and three missing people. We met with others at an appointed time and place and with buckets and shovels, removed the mud bit by bit, bucket by bucket. The top priority was to clear the debris from the closed highway. Until this was done, those needing to get into the area had to travel by ferry. Commercial fishing and whale-watching boats became temporary commuter ferries. In the first few weeks, there were hundreds of volunteers. Items were found like a closed lunchbox with the food still inside and still fresh. Eventually, the volunteers moved toward the storm drain area and the ravine where everything swept down the mountain. The landscape was so altered it was hard to tell where "the place" was at first, but the tree on the upper highway was still standing and was looking like it would survive to forever mark the place for me. I focused my efforts on recovery at the bottom of the ravine. It was tedious and slow work, but rewarding when something of value or sentiment was found.

People had lost everything, in some cases family members, so any little saved item took on great significance. The survivors whose homes had been washed away were given private access to a website where each recovered item was posted with a basic description and a photo. We were told to post absolutely anything salvageable. Julia found an intact ziplock bag of old love letters perfectly preserved. A volunteer found a jewelry box with one pearl earring caught in the lining. I found a baptism candle and a satin pouch of baby teeth. Numerous pieces of human lives were turned upside down by this unexpected tragedy, almost made worse by the fact that all these people had survived the devastating fires, only to succumb to and be buried in mud.

Two weeks in, it was getting more difficult to dig through the drying muck. A younger guy, probably one of the college student volunteers, called me over to help him remove something from the dirt.

"I think it's an old raincoat," he said. And it was. An old vintage yellow raincoat with buckles down the front. We carefully pulled it out, as I tried to maintain my composure. There was a tear near the bottom right side with a piece missing. We cleaned it off, labeled it, and posted it to the site so someone could claim it. I kept checking the website.

A young man responded. He claimed the jacket was his grandfather's. His grandpa's house was on the upper mountain very near the top, and was completely pulled off its foundation and sent down the hill during the slide. No one occupied the house at the time. The kid and his family were in the middle of sorting through a lifetime of belongings while the old man lived out his days in a local retirement nursing home. I sent the kid, Troy Pinkerton, a message asking if he wouldn't mind meeting with me. He agreed and asked to meet The Regency, an opulent, well-known retirement home.

"I can meet you between the lunch and dinner rush. I'm a

waiter," he explained.

I had to ring a doorbell and be buzzed in, then sign in. Troy met me in the lobby. He wore dark jeans, black Doc Marten boots, and a tight black t-shirt with a fish logo of a popular restaurant. His hair was dark and too long and he had a bull ring in his nose. He walked over, holding out his hand.

"I'm Troy. You must be Duncan."

"Call me Knight," I said.

"Cool."

I liked him instantly. I wondered how I could quickly steer the conversation to his grandfather and the jacket, but no worries, as it turned out, this is a kid who likes to talk. We sat on one of the overstuffed sofas in the formal lobby area.

"My grandpa lived up on the mountain forever. I didn't know him well as a kid. In fact, I only saw him a few times. There was always this air of secrecy about him and really that whole side of the family. Well, now I know it's because he's an asshole, a seriously grouchy old man. He's my mom's father, and he was mean to her and never liked her choice of a husband, my dad. In fact, his big threat was always that he would cut my mom off if she married him or if she voted a certain way, chose a certain career, or named her kids certain names. Just constant threats. My mom finally realized how toxic the relationship was and that she didn't need his financial help or care about an inheritance."

"So how'd you finally meet him?" I asked.

"Grandpa started getting into trouble in the nineties for stuff like disturbing the peace, firing his gun on his property, assaulting a lady in the grocery store, things like that. My mom thinks he may have started losing it, mentally, ya know? That's around the time she cut ties with him and did not make an effort for me to get to know him. She thought it was best. The only thing is, he has no other relatives, so any time he would get into trouble, she was called, either by him or his attorney. Then about two years ago he was found starving and not knowing who he was. Kids snuck onto his property and saw him, realized he was in awful shape, and thankfully had the wherewithal to call the police. Oh, yeah, about his property. It was overgrown, and it was kind of a thing that kids liked to dare each other to enter. Pretty dangerous, considering he carried his gun everywhere and had so many 'No Trespassing' signs. I can remember my buddies talking about sneaking onto the property when I was in high school, but I never went. Of course, I didn't realize it was my grandfather's property back then. He had an old outbuilding that they used to party in."

It occurred to me this was the same place Dad and I had been to for the survey. The man we met must be the kid's grandfather.

"It sounds like the same place my friends and I would party at back in the day." Hearing the kid's description, and remembering the property myself, I was confident it was. I explained.

"We used to hike up behind the property and we set up a pretty cool hangout in an old outbuilding that had a little corral around it, probably for a pony or some goats. The inside was just a stall connected to a storage area. There were some old buckets we used for seats, then later we had a box of blankets and a crate filled with candles and matches. I remember those cheap glass candles like you see at roadside memorials. Drinking beers or whatever alcohol someone swiped from their parents' stash, occasionally sharing a joint and just sitting around telling stories, waiting for ghosts in the glow of the candles. Harmless fun."

"Yup, definitely it was Grandpa's place," Troy nodded and continued, "So after they found him half dead and incoherent, he was brought here to stay in a safe place with supervision. Three decent meals in the dining hall or your room, cards, field trips, yoga, movie nights. It's pretty great. Mom's been paying the bills out of Grandpa's estate, which is sizeable, and which she'll inherit after all, ha ha, whatever is left of it that is, after paying the rent and care at this place, and she tasked me with going through his house to get it ready to sell once we knew it wouldn't be an option for him to go back. Then the fires, which his home miraculously survived. Then the slide, which it did not survive. And here we are. I recognized the jacket because I had just found it before the mudslide, that's how I knew it was his. He fished professionally for a while. He owned a few jackets in that style. I was hoping to learn more about him, maybe find old journals or papers, but now I'll never get the chance unless more items of his are recovered."

"How is his health these days?" I asked. "Will he talk to you?"

"Not too good, but he still manages to be mean as ever. You'd think a bit of remorse or repentance would be in order, but that's not who he is. I keep trying to ask about his life, but he accuses me of prying and tells me to, 'Get the hell out before I throw you out.' I try to be as gracious as I can. After all, Regency is a Memory Care Facility, and the protocol is to not upset the patients. They encourage us to listen and agree, keep it pleasant. There is no point in trying to correct a faulty memory. It just makes the residents agitated and gets you nowhere."

"I can understand that. Hey, would you mind if I meet

him? I'd love to try to talk with him. I'm a realtor, and I'm interested in the area's history."

"No, not at all, but don't say I didn't warn you. And if you have any luck, would you mind sharing with me? He was napping when I got here. He might be up now. I have to get back to work, but you could ask the front desk receptionist."

"I'll do that, and Troy, thanks for meeting with me. I'll be in touch either way to let you know how it went. Maybe we'll find more of his belongings too, you never know. Wait, what's his name?"

"It's Douglas Kerigan you'll want to ask for. He'll insist you call him Sergeant though or, as I said, he'll kick your ass straight out before you can say anything," Troy laughed at his own joke.

"Yes. 'Mr. Kerigan', thanks again. I'll get back to you after I meet with him."

I recalled the name from my previous encounter and I didn't have high hopes for my interview with Sergeant Douglas Kerigan, but figured I'd give it a shot. I checked with the front desk and was told he was still napping and to come back another day.

I planned an early afternoon visit, after lunch, but before dinner, hoping to catch him in a decent, lucid mood. The receptionist buzzed me into the lobby and I asked if I might see him.

"Sure, let me tell you where to find him."

I heard a couple clicks of her mouse, and she turned her monitor so I could see it. There was a map of the facility and a green blinking dot showed up in the outside garden area.

"He's here," she said, pointing at the flashing dot.

"You track them?" I asked.

"Yes, each of our residents has a bracelet. It's for their own

170

security and safety. They are free to enjoy the grounds, but can't wander off. That's why we have to buzz you in. Just sign here and you can go see him. Please remember not to upset him."

"I won't." At least I didn't plan to.

Instead of approaching him outright, I walked near and checked him out. He stood near the edge of the duck pond. He wore old navy blue Dickies with a leather belt and a black t-shirt tucked in tight. The shirt had a logo on the back for Chip's Plumbing Supplies. He had on white socks with slip-on sandals and a Dodgers baseball cap with a rim of snow-white hair showing beneath. He appeared to be like any mellow older guy. I decided to give it a try and speak to him.

"Mr. Kerigan? Sergeant? My name is Duncan Knight. I came to speak with you."

He sized me up, then walked over and sat on a wooden bench seat. I was encouraged and approached him.

"Mind if I sit?"

"Not against the law, as far as I know. Now, who are you, Boy?"

"I'm Duncan Knight, Sir. We've actually not met before. I'm a Real Estate agent from your neighborhood. I know your grandson." I was certain and correct in assuming he would have no memory of me from our brief encounter years before.

"So you're a crook!" With this, he laughed maniacally, and added, "What grandson?"

"Troy," I responded in a neutral tone.

"Don't remember the name. I believe I have a daughter, though, Marcy. Don't see much of her. Ran off and broke her Mom's heart. Wouldn't surprise me if she had a kid. Probably not married either. She was always troubled, that one."

I pulled the yellow raincoat from my bag. Troy had said it would be ok if I asked his grandfather about it.

"Sergeant, is this your coat? Do you recognize it?"

"Give me that!" He grabbed it and clutched it to his chest. "Where the hell did you get this? Did you find Trudy? Where is she? Did she come back again? That dumb bitch. I thought she was dead." His eyes focused on some point beyond me. "Oh, Trudy, I love you."

What the heck? He seemed to be thoroughly mixed up and getting agitated. I was unsure where this was leading and I was clearly upsetting the old man, exactly what I was not supposed to do.

"I thought it was yours, Sir. Sorry, I can just take it back now. Here, let me take it back. There's no need to get upset." I reached gingerly for the jacket, but he was clutching it tightly.

"Course it's mine. I have several. I'm a professional fisherman, you idiot. I need this for the morning. There's a storm coming. I can feel it in the air."

"I feel it too. I hear the fishing's really good right now. I'll let you get ready for the morning. You probably have a lot to do, I imagine. Should I put the jacket in your room?"

"OK, yes. And you should leave now, David."

"It's Duncan, Sir."

"Whatever it is. Just go. I'm tired of the questions."

He handed back the jacket and seemed to zone out, staring into the garden. I decided not to push my luck any further than I already had.

"Well, have a nice day, Sergeant. I hope I'll see you again." And with that, I left.

I called Troy as promised to let him know how my visit

went, and that I still had the jacket and would return it to him. "He mentioned Trudy. Was that his wife? Your grandmother?"

"Yes," Troy said. "I never met her. She left him shortly after my mom left for college in 1985, I believe. My mom hasn't heard from her since. Mom thinks Grandma Trudy disappeared on purpose. I didn't specifically mention it before, and you may have already figured it out, but Grandpa is a very abusive person, was, and still is. My mom doesn't like to talk about it. She was glad to get out and move away for college. I know she's hurt that her mother never tried to contact her, but she says she understands and feels some responsibility for leaving her mother alone with him. She tried to find her, but never could. Grandpa claims he has no idea where she went."

"Wow. That's rough." I didn't know what else to say.

"It doesn't affect me much, but I'm concerned about my mom. I know it bothers her, even though she doesn't talk about it. Maybe you could find out more about my grandmother. At least he was willing to speak to you."

"Sure, I can do that." After the old man's reaction to the jacket, I was curious to find out more and was glad to have Troy's encouragement to do so.

The next time I visited The Regency, I was signed in by one of the daytime staff.

"Oh, you're Duncan? Sergeant, Mr. Kerigan, will be excited to see you. He's been asking for you to come."

"Really? I've only met him the one time. He doesn't know me." The young nurse looked at me.

"Interesting. He may have you confused with someone from his past, but this is the most lucid I've seen him. He's not usually talkative, and when he is, he's very angry. Remember not to upset him. Just go with what he says."

173

"Will do. Is that him on the sofa?"

"Yes, I'll leave you to it. Good luck."

I approached the sofa, unsure of what to expect. The old man looked swallowed up by the plush cushions. He didn't have a hat today, and I could see he was bald on the top of his head. The local news was playing on a large TV screen, but his eyes were focused to the left, looking outside. *Will he show his mean side, or will I be able to have a conversation today?*

"Hi Sergeant, I've come to have a visit if that's alright with you. We met before. I'm Duncan Knight, do you remember me?" Whoops. I'd been told specifically by the nurses not to ask, 'Do you remember?' It tends to cause some people in the early stages of dementia to become defensive and accusatory as if you are purposely trying to trip them up.

"You're not Duncan. Duncan helped me with stuff. Or was that David? Remember secret things we can't talk about? You're not him!" His voice volume was rising, and I was sure I'd be politely asked to leave by a staff member. I thought quickly and went with it. I lowered my voice conspiratorially and leaned in.

"Yes, of course. I helped you with a lot of things." May as well try to find out what, so I asked, "What were the things I helped with?"

"You know perfectly well what, you moron. You think I'm gonna say stuff out loud? People could be listening. I know better than that." He dropped his voice. "You did the search for me. And brought me the jacket. Then I owed you, so I let you stay out back. Sure, you were helpful, but I've paid you back. I don't owe you anything."

"Yes, thank you Sir. I was always glad to help."

"You chased the kids off too and anyone else who came

poking around. And you took the rap for firing the gun that time. You're a good kid, David. A good kid. Like a Son I never had."

"Sergeant, can we talk about Trudy?"

Then he bent forward with his head in his hands, and great sobs shook him. I caused this and wasn't sure quite what to do. I rested a hand on his back and rubbed it gently, saying, "Trudy must have been a lovely lady."

"Oh, she was. She was. She is. So beautiful, the best wife any man could have. Why did she leave me? Why is she gone?"

He looked up and implored, "Do you know Trudy? Can you bring her here? I miss her. Will you bring her?"

I rubbed his back a few more times and said, "I'll try, Sir. I'm going to say goodbye now. Maybe you need to take a rest in your room."

"Yes, that's what I'll do while I wait for my Trudy."

I left the building, got into my car, and turned on the engine and the AC. I called Troy. He didn't pick up but called back just as I pulled into my office parking lot.

"Hey, Knight, sorry I missed the call. What's up? Did you go to see Grandpa? Did he talk to you?"

"I didn't learn a lot. I think he was really confused about the year. He said he missed Trudy and wanted to see her again and could I please bring her to see him."

"Yeah, he's mixed up about time. Sometimes he knows me as a grandson and other times, he doesn't know me at all. Dementia is a trip. I hope I never get it."

"He kept mentioning David. Do you know who that is?"

"That's this shady guy who was a sort of caretaker. He did odd jobs for Grandpa. I saw him a few times. Super weird, not friendly. A transient, really. I think Grandpa would let him stay in the shed. I can ask my mom. She might know more."

I continue to visit the Sergeant. He seldom speaks at all, but I've been showing up with a checkers set, and he'll play a game or two. Sometimes, he stands and walks away mid-game. Then I pack up and leave. I don't know what I expect from the visits, but I don't mind going.

The grounds are beautiful at The Regency and I don't imagine the Sergeant receives many visitors besides me. Troy and his mom appreciate that I go. Troy is busy and only visits about once a month and his Mom is an hour away, so she rarely sees her father. It must frustrate her to travel an hour and then feel shut out if the Sergeant is having one of his quiet days and won't talk or acknowledge her at all. I try to ask him questions, but I've learned very little. If he speaks to me, it's about his days in the service and the pranks he and his buddies played on each other. He says how beautiful Trudy is, expresses disappointment in his daughter, Marcy, if he remembers her at all, and shuts down the conversation completely or gets angry and nasty if he thinks I am prying for details.

Then he tells me to, "Get the hell out of here and don't come back."

And I respond, "Okay Sarge, I'll see you next time," and take my leave.

2016

I T NEVER BOTHERED ME that Julia and I couldn't have children, except for the fact that I knew it upset her, and that she would be an amazing mother if afforded the chance. We spoke of maybe fostering a child or adopting one, but we never looked into it. And suddenly we were in our 40s. To be honest, I considered my life perfectly full. I have my job and work commitments, my wife, parents, our dogs and foster dogs and a comfortable, predictable, some might even say, boring, life. Then one Sunday morning, Julia was very distressed. She was sitting cross-legged on the sofa in our room with her laptop open, and she was crying.

"Why are you crying? Honey, what is wrong?"

Julia is not one to get overly emotional, so I was on guard and braced myself for something terrible.

"Apparently, according to all the overwhelming evidence on the internet, I am in perimenopause! Which means I am a washed up old hag, and my best years are behind me. I knew this day would come, but I'm 43. I mean, come on, I thought I had a few years left at least."

Julia tended to get over dramatic about things like this, but she looked miserable. I wanted to speak the right words and went with, "Well, maybe it's a blessing. You won't have to deal with those awful periods anymore." Bad choice. She asked me to leave then. Not permanently. She just would rather not see my face or say something mean to me that she'd later regret. I respected her wishes, took two dogs, and left to walk the beach and run errands. I stopped in to visit the Sergeant. He was pretty out of it. I didn't mind. It is during these times I can speak freely of my troubles and he just stares vacantly, or offers a perfunctory groan from time to time.

"Julia and I are getting older, Sarge, and it feels weird. When did this happen? Why haven't I noticed?" I wondered aloud, not expecting a response.

In a moment of clarity, the Sergeant said, "Well, at least you have your wife to get old with. Who knows when I'll see Trudy again?"

"I'm sorry Sir, you're right. I need to appreciate my beautiful wife and enjoy every minute."

"That you do, Son," he responded, and I took my leave while he was peaceful and in a quiet state of mind.

I came home later with a mixed bouquet and Julia and I relaxed in the jacuzzi. Julia said she had called in sick for the next day to clear her head and was going to see her doctor for a checkup and might call her best friend. I knew it was serious. As a teacher, she never calls in sick because that means writing lesson plans for a substitute teacher, which she has made clear many times is far more difficult and time-consuming than just going in to teach her class.

"Do you want me to stay home too? Keep you company?" I asked tentatively.

"No, not necessary. I know I'm being a brat about this, but I need to mourn the loss of my youth alone. Please, just let me be dramatic."

The next day, she texts me at work asking if I'm free for lunch. "Of course," I say, and meet her at our favorite, Village Coffee. We sat at a little table on the patio by the bougainvillea.

She grabs my hands in hers and looks me dead in the eyes and says, "We are having a baby."

"Who is having a baby, Jules?"

"We are having a baby."

This is exactly how she told me. I could feel the electricity in her hands. I was completely overwhelmed. Stunned. We had let that dream go. I had held her so many times while she cried it out after attending a baby shower or after holding the newborn of one of her students' families. This was why we had filled our lives and home with babies of the fur variety.

"Let's go to that fancy baby store right now." The one we avoided every time we walked past.

"Yes," she said, unable to hide the excitement in her voice. We got our coffees to go.

Julia's was a decaf.

"I'll be needing to give up my coffee habit." I could hear the glee in her voice. The store was on the same block and was only a few minutes walk. We entered, opening the bottom half of a dutch door, and stood in wonder.

"Can I help you?" The saleslady approached us from the back of the shop.

"We're just looking. But we are having a baby, in…" I turned to Julia, realizing I didn't even know when this miracle was due to arrive.

"June," Julia was smiling from ear to ear.

"We just found out," I explained to the saleslady, "so we honestly do not know what we're looking for, or what we'll even need for our baby."

"Our baby," I whispered softly, marveling at how easy and natural the words seemed. The store held a dizzying array of products, and I resisted the urge to buy one of everything.

"I'll be here to help, whenever you're ready, or if you have any questions," the saleslady assured us, "and, Congratulations!"

"Thanks, we couldn't be happier," Julia gushed, "and we'll come back when we're a little further along."

We left with the tiniest, perfect, handmade, and obscenely expensive white cardigan, and headed home to share the news with Mom and Dad. They were beyond thrilled.

"This is the best possible news ever! You two will be wonderful parents. A grandbaby, oh I can't wait." Turning to Julia, "When are you due?"

"The doctor said June or July. We'll know more at the next appointment."

My parents' marriage had taken a similar path. Mom and Dad wanted children from the start, but circumstances had granted them only me. Until I knew Julia was pregnant, I never allowed myself the thought of being a father, but the minute I knew, it was as if it was all I'd ever wanted. I did not want Julia to go to work or even leave my sight, but I couldn't let her know this. I had to swallow it down and deal with the anxiety each time we were apart until I saw her again. I sent multiple texts a day but was careful to space them. I did not want to barrage her or have her worry about me worrying about her. If someone was targeting me, would they mess with her?

Julia experienced occasional morning sickness at the beginning and some extreme fatigue, but overall, everything was going well. She was seen by her doctor often, was taking a prenatal yoga class at the gym, and was getting into the nesting phase, which meant the seldom-used guest room located next to our room was being transformed into a perfect nursery. I suggested she take a leave from her job, but she insisted she could finish the year. The students were an amiable group. At 20 weeks we went in for an ultrasound and some blood work. Julia's doctor was monitoring her closely, this being her first pregnancy, and she was considered high-risk due to her age. The blood work was for a multiple marker test to screen for birth defects such as Spina Bifida or a type of Down Syndrome, more common in babies whose mothers are older.

Turns out the baby had a marker for possible Down Syndrome and an amniotic fluid test could let us know for certain. But with that test came a 3% chance of miscarriage. We opted not to have the test; 3% was not worth it. All we wanted in the world was for our baby to be healthy, but whatever the outcome was, we would handle it and love our baby, regardless. It simply wasn't an option to risk a miscarriage. And what if our baby had a birth defect, would knowing that change our minds to continue the pregnancy? No. Julia would have more ultrasounds than usual, and each time the doctor seemed secure that all was well. And each time he asked if we would like to know whether we were having a boy or girl. We declined, but had fun scrutinizing the films and trying to figure it out ourselves.

Dad and I painted the nursery a soft mocha shade. Before we began, I needed to clear out the closet, which we used as storage, requiring me to move the yellow slicker. I'd hung it in the back of the guest closet, inside a garment bag, when the pool house was turned into the rescue office, and I'd all but forgotten it. Why was I keeping it? What purpose did it serve other than to taunt me and force me to replay the worst night of my life? It couldn't be the same jacket from the incident. That was impossible, but I felt inexplicably obligated to hang onto it. I moved it to my half of our walk-in closet. The fortune and the bit of rubberized fabric were securely hidden beneath the bottom drawer of my dresser and could only be accessed by removing the drawer completely. From time to time, I checked and scrutinized if they'd moved, even though I knew they hadn't. Sometimes I fantasized that the fire had destroyed our home and the evidence of my possible crime right along with it. The old journal lived there too, under the drawer. It remained the only written record of what I believe may have happened that night. I should dispose of all these items and wipe the incident clean from my memory. If only there was a way to do it. I've since started a new journal. I only write hints of the torture I feel. I vaguely describe my anxiety, nothing anyone could draw conclusions from, nothing damning. *Do I keep my old journal so I can be found out eventually and taken to task for what I did?* Now that I'm going to be a father... My family needs to come first. I need to protect them at all costs.

2017

ELLE MARIE KNIGHT WAS born in May, six weeks early but weighing in at a healthy 5 pounds even. She was kept in the NICU for a week to be sure her lungs were developed enough. Visitors could get a peek of her through the thick glass of the NICU, but only Julia and I were allowed in the room to hold and rock her. She took to nursing like a champ, and I was, and am, in awe of Julia. When the day came to take Elle home, we celebrated with the nurses, bringing them each boxes of fancy chocolates and gift certificates to a local steak house. We dressed baby Elle in a tiny soft beige one piece with a small matching beanie on her head and the white cardigan we had bought when we first knew Julia was pregnant.

"It's a shame you kept missing your brother when he was here," one of the nurses remarked, "I'm sure you'll all gather together now that you can bring Elle home."

I felt my skin crawl, but kept my voice level, and asked, "What do you mean? I don't have any siblings."

"Oh, I'm sorry. There was a man who kept coming by to

see the baby. He said he was her uncle."

"What does he look like?" I demanded, sounding harsher than I intended. "And what do you mean when you say, 'kept coming by?' How many times has he shown up here?"

"I'm sorry, Mr. Knight. I didn't mean to upset you. I'm sure I misunderstood. He must have been here to see a different baby. Please accept my apologies."

"Well, who was he then? What did he look like?" I was struggling to keep the edge out of my tone.

"I don't really know. He has brown hair that he wore in a ponytail, kinda scruffy I guess, average height," she trailed off. "I'm sorry. I really don't know. I obviously made a mistake. Sorry."

"It's okay," Julia said. "I'm sure it was just a mistake. Thank you for all you've done for us. We appreciate your dedication."

"Yes. Thank you," I agreed. There was no point in me pushing this nurse for information. A lot of visitors came through. Why do I always have to overreact? I wanted nothing to dampen the excitement and joy of bringing my daughter home.

Julia strapped Elle into the car seat. Elle was so tiny it looked as if she needed a smaller one. We left the NICU. In the elevator, I quizzed Julia, trying not to be too obvious.

"What other babies have been in the NICU with Elle?"

"Those two little boys. I met the mom. They're twins."

"So, there weren't any other baby girls?"

"No. Duncan, what are you getting at? Do you think someone visited that didn't belong? That makes no sense. Don't get worked up over nothing. You were a little intimidating to the nurse. She was only trying to make polite conversation."

"You're probably right," I agreed. "I just don't want to think of some stranger looking at our baby."

"I know. But Duncan, I've looked at babies through the glass before. Every time I've ever visited anyone in the hospital, I go to look at the babies. Sometimes people just want to see babies. Babies make everyone happy. The guy was probably the twin babies' uncle. It's not a big deal, really. You don't think we should worry, do you?"

"No, no, I'm overreacting, you know how I get. I just want to protect my girls, that's all." If Julia wasn't worried, then I shouldn't be either, I reasoned.

The next few weeks were a time to settle in as new parents. I spent much more time at home than usual. Julia would not go back to work until fall, and maybe not even then. We would need to decide.

I am keeping my demons at bay, but the nightmares have begun again. The dark night, the flash of yellow, the falling. Sometimes it is me who is falling. Other times, I am a witness to a falling body. I'm running. I'm being chased. All I know is if I can outrun whatever is chasing me, I can be free. Then I'm up against the guardrail. I see the tree. It's swaying, looking like it's going to uproot itself, but there is no wind. The guardrail bends with my weight. I feel hands pushing me. Something or someone wants me to plummet over the edge. I push back and feel a solid body and I scream, "NO!"

Then I'm in bed, sitting bolt upright and soaked in my own sweat. The baby is crying. Julia isn't here. She's with Elle comforting her and rushing back to me to see what made me scream. She enters the room holding Elle and is followed by a pack of dogs. The dogs crowd next to me. They smell my sweat. They smell my fear. I know if they could, they'd tell me I'll be okay. Everything will be okay.

"What is it? Duncan, are you alright?"

"Oh, God. I'm sorry, Babe. Bad dream. Where were you?"

"I was up with Elle. She was wet and needed to be fed. I heard you scream." She cradled Elle in the crook of one arm and put her other arm around my shoulders in an attempt to comfort me.

"Same dream?"

I have only shared that I have a recurring dream of falling, no other details. There have times I've wanted to tell Julia everything, but something holds me back. *Would she still love me?* "Yes, the same one."

Julia sits next to me. Elle is swaddled, with only her little face showing. I reach for her and am instantly calm, holding her small warm body, taking in her baby scent. I have my wife, my daughter, my parents close by and my trusty dogs. I have nothing to fear.

Weeks and months go by, time measured by each new developmental milestone of our little girl. I finally under-stand why people say, "Someone, slow down time," when they talk about their children, and how things change, "in the blink of an eye." Julia did not go back to work after the summer. Elle was only three and a half months old. Instead, she applied for an extended leave of absence. Her school district would save her a position for a year. She was fully embracing motherhood, joining classes for babies, and meeting other new moms. I insisted she have her phone at all times and send me regular updates throughout the day. My schedule was flexible enough to spend a lot of time with them, and much of my paperwork I brought home to do rather than stay at the office. I encouraged Julia to take a dog along whenever they went to the park or the beach or for a walk and to carry pepper spray.

2018

Two significant milestones happened on Elle's first birthday. She took her first uneasy steps without holding onto one of the taller dogs, and she spoke her first word, "dog." I tried to claim it was "Dad," but we all heard the drawn out "o" sound and knew it was "dog." It made perfect sense. Elle was with the dogs from morning to night, crawling into their beds, tugging on their fur, stealing their toys, but also sharing hers. One or more constantly guarded her. She and the dogs seemed to communicate and have an understanding that at no time was she to be left without at least one dog on watch. Under the highchair, next to the crib, even by the tub at bath time, a dog was always there. We were careful with the temporary fosters, never sure how they would act with a baby, but the pack let the newcomers know really quickly that the child was not to be messed with. Ever.

Julia invited a few friends from her "Mommy and Me" class who brought their babies along to celebrate Elle's birthday. I tried my best to keep their names and their children's names straight. Besides Elle, all babies look alike to me. I am biased, of course, but Elle is the most beautiful little girl I've ever seen.

Mom and Julia chose a dog themed party because Elle is all about the dogs. The weather was clear and calm, a balmy spring day. Off the back deck on the grass area, Mom and Julia spread out rainbow colored blankets shaded by a rented pop up sun shade. There was a baby pool filled with multi-colored balls, a sandbox with shovels and pails, a water table and a bubble machine. The dogs were kept in one of the bigger yards during the festivities. Dad barbecued chicken and there was a spread of green salad, potato salad and rolls, along with baby friendly finger foods for the little guests, and, of course, cupcakes and chocolate chip cookies.

"Time to open gifts before everyone needs a nap," Julia announced. Elle was handed one wrapped present at a time and relished tearing off the paper, some of it ending up in her mouth. All the babies "helped" with the gift opening and tried out the new toys, while moms and dads snapped photos on their phones and remarked over the fun new toys and tiny clothing.

"Here's one more," Mom said, and handed me a wrapped box. I felt my pulse quicken when she said, "It was left on our porch this morning. It's probably from one of Elle's little friends who couldn't make it. Isn't her little friend Heidi not here?"

"Thanks Mom, maybe she can open it later." I didn't like hearing that it was left on the porch, and instantly felt concerned.

"Oh, let's just let her have it. She's having so much fun opening presents."

And before I knew it, Elle was tearing the wrapping off

the latest box as Julia lifted the lid. She pulled out a small child size yellow raincoat, as my heart sank and I struggled not to pass out.

"That is so cute! It's a little yellow slicker! A tiny raincoat!" Mom said, reaching for it.

"I don't see a card," Julia said.

Of course you don't.

"Oh, here it is." She pulled a card out of the box, silently reading the front. Opening it, and gasping, she handed the card to me. I saw the puppies on the front with a giant number one and opened the card to reveal a printed message I didn't read. My eyes went straight to the hand-written words in blue ink, "From Your Uncle."

"We can talk about this after the guests leave," Julia whispered.

"Yes," I agreed, making an effort to keep my voice neutral and calm as my stomach clenched.

Babies and parents ate cupcakes, and then we wrapped up the festivities. The entire party took just under two and a half hours. Babies were exhausted and ready for naps before meltdowns began. We said our goodbyes, and after settling Elle down for her nap, Julia and I could finally talk. We never told my parents about the "visiting uncle" at the hospital, but shared it with them after the party. We wanted their opinions.

"I mean, we weren't concerned then," Julia said. "We didn't want to worry you. We figured it was a misunderstanding." Her voice was shaky. "Do you think we should call the sheriff?" Julia asked.

My parents didn't answer, but looks of alarm crossed their faces.

"But what would that sound like? The nurse at the hospital said a guy claimed to be Elle's uncle and looked at her twice through the glass. Then there's been nothing suspicious over the past year that we know of. Then this gift shows up signed by an 'Uncle'. What will that sound like?" Julia asked again. She was trying to convince herself she was overreacting. I knew the feeling.

"What about Sheriff Shiloh?" Dad said. "You guys know him. You could run it past him, ask him if he thinks there's a reason for concern."

"That would at least put it on his radar," Mom agreed.

"I'll call him tomorrow," I said, keeping my voice even. *And I won't sleep tonight.*

After our meeting on the beach, Sheriff Shiloh and his family had adopted a beautiful spaniel mixed breed from our rescue. We'd run into each other occasionally at Village Coffee.

Other times we'd see him at the beach with our kids and dogs. I felt confident calling him for an opinion. It was the prudent thing to do. I called the next day, and he stopped in at our home that evening during his shift. We explained the situation, Julia adding, "I know we're overreacting, but it just feels a little creepy."

"Not at all. I'm glad you called. I'll take a report, and that way, if anything else suspicious comes up, we'll have a record." Then he added, "There's no one you suspect, right? No one who has a grudge against you?" *Was he looking at me?*

"No, of course not," Julia said. "Duncan used to get graffiti on his photo ads, but that was years ago, and just high schoolers trying to be funny, right?"

I was thankful that particular prank seemed to have stopped, but I also wasn't paying for photo ads on benches anymore.

In a moment of inspiration, I blurted, "Do you think I should have a gun? Just to be safe?"

"Well, that's up to you. If you do purchase a weapon, I suggest you get some training on how to use it and store it safely. When inexperienced folks buy guns, the chance of an accident isn't worth it. Training is everything," he emphasized and added, "You may want to get some security cameras around the property. That way, if someone tries to leave a package again, we'll know who it is."

We thanked him for his time, and I privately vowed to look into gun ownership the next day.

"I'm not sure how I feel about a gun in the house, Duncan," Julia said that night as we lay in bed.

"Wouldn't it be better just to get cameras and a decent alarm system?"

We'd talked about it for years, but never installed a security system, figuring that someone was usually home and it was a low crime area, and we had the dogs who alerted us to any suspicious activity.

"I hear you, Honey, but if someone ever threatened us or Elle, I'd like protection. If the other person had a gun and I didn't, I couldn't protect us." I didn't press the issue.

2019

Though I know it to be true, I cannot get my head around this reality. I don't remember my grandparents. Mom's parents died before I was born. I only briefly knew Dad's parents. They passed away within six months of each other, and I was too young to grieve for them. I didn't know them. If I didn't consider myself the man of the house before, now I have no choice. I'm not ready. I'm not prepared. Dad was fine, his usual self. Or is that me just wanting it to be so?

Too wrapped up in my own life to recognize there were signs.

I came home from the office at four, changed into trunks, and joined Julia and Elle in the pool. It was unseasonably warm for February, and we heated the pool to 82 degrees, which was the same temperature as the outside air.

"Where's Dad?" I'd asked. "I thought he'd be out here too. I saw his car."

Mom looked up from under her floppy sun hat. She was absorbed in her book, lounging in one of the teak Adirondack chairs.

"He came home early. Headache. He went to lie down. Let's leave him be. I'll check if he's up to having dinner later."

"Sounds good," I replied, and put it out of my mind, just splashing and enjoying my time with Julia and Elle. Elle is a water baby, and I can picture teaching her to surf in just a few years. Around six, we dried off and came inside. We pulled sandwich makings out of the fridge: romaine, dark brown bread, spicy mustard, avocado, spouts, provolone, and sliced turkey. Mom made Dad's favorite potato salad earlier in the day, German, without mayonnaise. With cold sparkling water, it was a perfect meal. No one felt like turning on the oven or stovetop.

"Should we wake up Dad?" Julia asked.

"Let's let him sleep," Mom replied. "His head was really hurting. I think he might be fighting a cold or something."

After dinner, Julia and I read stories to Elle and put her to bed in her crib. She was worn out from the pool and had skipped her nap.

In the family room, Mom was reading her novel and watching the news. Then she said, "I'm off to shower. I'll check on your father, see if he's feeling better." About 20 minutes later, Mom called out. It was a scream. A long drawn-out, "Noooooo!" I sensed the desperation and instantly feared the worst. "Duncan, Julia, come quick."

We ran into my parents' room, followed by the dogs. Mom was in her robe with her hair wrapped up in a towel. She was sitting on the edge of the bed and shaking, holding Dad's hand. The dogs whimpered and whined.

"He's gone." It was barely a whisper and filled with pain.

"What do you mean? What are you talking about? Not Dad." I would not accept it.

"Yes. I spoke to him, said to start waking up while I

showered, that I'd fix him a sandwich when I got out. I didn't hear him reply, but I didn't check on him until I got out. I thought he was still asleep."

We sat next to Mom. I didn't want to look closely, but I had to. Dad's eyes were closed as if asleep, but he was pale and unnatural looking. The blood had drained from his face. I touched his hand. It wasn't stiff, but it felt cool. He was gone. I knew it even before I checked his pulse.

We found out later it was a stroke. There wasn't anything we could have done. He probably never felt a thing. Just went to sleep peacefully and didn't wake up.

Though we were all in shock, Julia took the lead in planning his service and memorial. He wanted to be cremated and his ashes scattered on our property. It forced me to think of my mortality, and I knew I'd want the same when my time came. We would preserve some of Dad's ashes in a blown glass art sculpture. Only weeks before, Dad pointed out an ad for turning your loved one's ashes into art. He'd help up the photo, declaring, "This. This is what I want you to do with my ashes. Scatter some on our property, and make one of these sculptures with the rest."

"You got it, Chief," I'd joked.

Messages, cards, flowers, and fruit baskets flowed in as soon as the word spread of his passing. Many loved Charles, "Chuck" Knight. The day of the service arrived, and I smelled the flowers before I entered the church. Wreaths on stands and other arrangements covered the altar. I wondered who had sent each one. Friends? Clients? Colleagues? Dad had always enjoyed a robust social life. He and Mom each have their own circle of friends, plus many that intersect. If the stacks of Christmas cards are any sign- I should have known how crowded his memorial would be. Every

Christmas, Mom tapes up all the cards they receive, creating a patchwork display that encompasses one entire wall of our dining room. Many of them are from my friends. I glance at their family portraits barely registering who they are and how many kids they have, and how the kids have grown. I grow bored reading the obligatory newsletter reporting on Science Fair ribbons and college acceptances and sports teams. Yet, since becoming a parent, I look forward to creating our own Christmas letter informing the world about any and every milestone of Elle's. There is nothing more important. I get it now. I get it that this is how my parents feel about me. That even as an adult, they revel in my accomplishments, they do anything they can for me and always have. I finally understand now, but I wonder if I would, if I'd never had the chance to be a parent.

I sat in the pew and listened to the readings we chose, trying desperately to hold back my tears and battling self-doubt. Was I good enough for my dad? Deserving enough? Did he know how much I loved and appreciated him? I hope my actions expressed my love clearly and that he left this world peacefully and is now with God. I felt Julia's hand squeeze into mine. Her other hand cradled Elle, who, still so tiny for her age, was asleep on Julia's chest in a baby carrier. Elle gently sucked her thumb, eyes closed in baby bliss. *Will she remember anything about her Papa?* I thought to myself. Grateful for the obscene amount of photos we have, I resisted the urge to pull out my phone and look at them right then, wanting to see Dad's smile as it was, wanting to see his expression as he looked at his granddaughter. The service ended, and I felt like I missed the whole thing, too caught up in my own thoughts to focus. We headed over to the reception in the church hall. I'm glad we arranged it to take place there and not at our house. There were so many people crowding in, friends of Dad's and Mom's, friends of mine. Even Troy showed up with the Sergeant. I was touched that so many cared, but so overwhelmed. I was thinking, *I can't deal with this many people. I'm uncomfortable,* but I shook hands with folks I've never met and listened to them say how sorry they were, how wonderful Dad was. Was. From now on I'll need to get used to referring to him in the past.

I need to find Mom, see how she's holding up. She seems fine. I know this is terrible for her, but she is surrounded with support and love.

Then a man I didn't recognize tapped my shoulder and said, "Duncan, you're needed outside. There's a group of homeless individuals that want to come in. I politely asked them to leave, but they wouldn't. They say they're waiting for your mother. They say they know her and want to pay their respects."

"Mom doesn't need this. Not today. I'll deal with it," I said.

I made my way to the front entrance of the community hall, dreading an altercation, anger simmering. When I exited, I saw a small group of about eight people gathered to the right of the entrance of the building. They were grubby and disheveled. Who knew if they were on drugs? One guy was clutching a bottle wrapped in a paper bag.

No. I am not letting them come into the hall. Not happening. I thought.

These were likely the same people who nap in the church and show up for handouts in this very building. I've contributed a fair amount of funding to this program. Not that I wanted to have these people at my Dad's memorial. Not that I wanted to actually be in personal contact with them. It's true, they probably know Mom since she volunteers here every week. All the same, it felt incredibly intrusive and inappropriate that they showed up. I walked over to the group and said, "Would you all mind leaving, please? This is a private event, and it's not appropriate that you're here." When no one budged, but they continued to stare at me, I said a little more forcefully, "I've asked you nicely. Please leave." A man, who I can only assume was the group's designated spokesperson, spoke up.

"We want to pay our respects to Linda. We know her husband passed away."

"That is very kind of you all. I will let her know. Now, as I've asked, please leave," I responded in a measured tone. Another man approached. As he got closer, I backed up. *He shouldn't be in my space. I don't want to look at him. I feel repulsed.*

He spoke up. "She means a lot to us. To me. She's like a mother to me."

That set me off. "She is not your mother. She is my mother. And you are not welcome here. Not today." I felt my anger boiling up, and I struggled to control myself. Why did these people feel entitled to my mom? They had no right to be here. "Please, please just leave," I implored. And they finally did, slowly picking up belongings, and one, pushing a shopping cart. As a group, they turned and moved away.

"Thank you," I called out. The last man who spoke held his palm up and turned his back to me, with his head hanging. After letting out a deep breath, I went back into the hall.

I joined Julia, half listening to friends of my father speaking on the microphone about all he meant to them. I only listened when Mom thanked everyone for coming and for their support. She said, "I know Chuck sees us all, and even though it feels way too soon to say goodbye, I know he will live on." I was glad when it was time to leave, preferring to process my grief in private, preferring to cry in the shower where no one could see.

Since then, each day is a tiny bit easier living without him. His presence is everywhere, and I feel him with me. We scattered his ashes near the willow tree. The sculpture arrived, and it sits in the kitchen window, its blue and yellow swirls reflecting the light. Lawyers are taking care of the practical stuff. His partners will fully take over the accounting firm but are keeping his name. We will still own the building. Troy has decided to get his CPA license and has begun an internship at Dad's office. Mom is doing well. She was busy before and still is. She is lonely and misses Dad, but isn't depressed, thank God. In fact, she has joined a women's travel group and will be taking a road trip to visit National Parks in three states.

Elle is thriving and still looks for and asks for her Papa. For that matter, the dogs still look too. We are settling into our new normal together.

2020

I T WAS JUNE. IT was hot. Julia and I took Elle to the beach. It's one of the few places we can feel normal besides our house, ever since March, when it felt like the entire world shut down. We've been careful to keep our contacts limited. I don't want to expose my mom to the virus and we still don't know too much about it. I'm grateful Elle is only three and too young to understand how strange the world is right now, how uneasy. Elle just knows she loves the ocean and since the last time we went, she's been relentless and has decided it's her favorite place. I remember the first time I took her by myself. I learned what a swim diaper was. She beelined, running on chubby legs, straight for the water to fill her pail and was totally soaked and pleased with herself. Her regular diaper blew up to three times the usual size. It was so funny. Now she asks to go every day, and if we can, Julia and I indulge her by loading the mesh bags of plastic toys into the car, along with towels and snacks and we drive down the hill to the protected little cove where all the parents of toddlers normally gather. Now, with guidelines on gatherings, everyone was careful to keep a respectful distance, even outside.

We spent three hours playing, splashing, and building a sand castle over and over so Elle could jump on it and smash it with her little feet. *This is what makes a life a life,* I thought. Julia offered to drive home, but I said I would drive and I purposely took the route where we'd pass the place. The sun was really bright and the windshield grimy and water spotted. I wanted to be done being plagued by what had happened or not, 25 years ago. Especially now with people dying from a contagious virus we know so little about, I need to focus on the present and be grateful for every minute and all that I have.

I am over this; I thought.

And then I took the familiar turn, at the same time realizing the date, June 10, and noticing the time 1:35pm lit in green on the dashboard. A car was pulled over to the side, up against the guardrail. It was an old beater that looked very much like my old car. A kid, who I guessed was in his early 20s, was leaning over the guardrail.

"Oh, my gosh! Honey, it looks like that boy is going to jump. Pull over. Stop the car. We need to help him," Julia shouted, panic rising in her voice. I pulled over.

"Stay here, Julia. I'll handle this. Don't worry."

"Be careful, Duncan."

From my perspective, he didn't look like he was about to jump. I saw a distraught young man and could feel in every fiber of my body what he was feeling, and it was sheer panic and dread. In my own head, I heard his shaky voice. *What have I done? I just killed someone.* I walked over to the car with as much calm as I could muster. I leaned down and saw that the right front side of his car was dented and just as I knew there would be, a piece of yellow rubber fabric was caught underneath. *What the hell?* I didn't know if I was hallucinating or if the past 25 years were ending in this sick and twisted culmination of fate. *Just what the hell?* This made no sense. But at the same time, it did.

I grabbed the boy by the waistband of his shorts and pulled him back and away from the guardrail. His eyes were wild, his face twisted and distraught. I could feel his heart pounding through his t-shirt. I could smell sweat and sunscreen and dread.

"It's Ok, It's Ok, It's Ok" I kept repeating.

"I think I hit someone. A woman, maybe. They just ran out in front of me. I couldn't stop. There was no way I could stop. Oh my God. Oh my God."

"What did you hit? What did you see?"

"I don't know. I'm not sure now. I think it was a lady, but maybe not. There was yellow, yellow clothing. Or was it the sun? I don't know. I don't know." His voice rose, shrill with nervousness.

A calm came over me, my eyes connected with his, and I spoke with gentle assurance. "What is your name?"

"It's Jesse." He was sobbing now. "I need to call the cops."

My hand was on his shoulder. I felt him shudder at the touch. I saw what he was experiencing in his mind: sitting in a jail cell, going to a trial, and being convicted of manslaughter. Years of his life passed by with frightening rapidity.

"Jesse. Listen to me. We can call the cops. I'll have my wife call. But, listen. You didn't hit someone." As I spoke, I knew it was true. The words were coming out spontaneously from deep within my conscience, and I was a listener along with Jesse.

"There is bad energy here. There is something evil about

this place. A tragedy that was never resolved, and it keeps playing out. You didn't cause it, but you are a part of it now. Years ago, I thought I hit something too. And in a way, we did, but we weren't the first and we won't be the last. We can make this stop. We can make this right." My own voice spoke to both of us, and I suspected what we needed to do next.

I walked back to my car and calmly asked Julia to take Elle home. "I'll stay here with Jesse. We'll figure this out. Go ahead home."

When Julia drove away, I asked Jesse to trust me. He agreed. He may have been in shock but was obviously thankful to have someone else take charge. He was relieved not to involve the police and to hear me tell him he would be okay. He was only a kid, just as I had been. I felt toward him as I might feel toward a son. I didn't want him to fret and suffer as I had for almost half my life. I wasn't sure what the outcome would be, but the voice, from someplace buried within my psyche, gave me clarity. I listened and followed my instincts.

As we stood by the guardrail next to the tree, I called Troy. I still pop in to visit Sergeant Kerigan occasionally. His memory is so faulty though, it's as if we start fresh every time. I don't know why I continue the visits. We typically just play a quick game of checkers and I leave. I know he has few visitors, and it isn't too much trouble for me. In the last few years, he's grown very quiet, but still I continue to go. Troy's number was in my contacts. I hoped he'd pick up. He did.

"Troy, it's Duncan. I need to ask you some questions about your Grandmother Trudy. It's important, urgent really."

"Sure, okay. What do you want to know?" It sounded like Troy was driving.

"Do you remember when your mom last saw her? Or if she ever was in touch after she left your grandfather?"

"No, my mom never saw her after she left for college. When Mom came back home, my grandfather told her Grandma Trudy had run away and left him. She could never track her down. I think she assumed my grandmother didn't want to be found. I told you this before. Why do you ask? Did you find out something?"

"I think your grandfather knows where your grandmother is. I'm heading over to see him if you want to meet me. I can explain more later."

"Well, you should probably know, he had a stroke early this morning. He's been moved to the hospital. Intensive Care. I was informed this morning. It's not looking good, and they suggested I gather any family members who may want to say their goodbyes. Actually, I'm just arriving at the hospital now. Mom's meeting me. I'll put your name on the list of approved visitors, but I'm not sure if they'll let you in. I was planning to call you after I got there. It's weird you called me." *You do not know how weird.*

"Thanks, I'm on my way." I turned to Jesse, "Can I drive your car?" He nodded.

On the short drive, Jesse spoke about how confused he felt. How he'd messed up his life, forgone college and now he was 22 with no plans. "And on top of it all, I might be a criminal, and none of this will matter if I'm rotting in a jail cell. What a waste. My life is over, and it never really began."

The feeling that I was, in fact, watching a version of my younger self was surreal and frightening. I had to keep my wits about me. I had to stay calm and figure this out. The pieces were starting to fit, but I still wasn't entirely sure if my instincts were right. I needed to speak with the Sergeant and

205

hoped he would be lucid enough for conversation.

"Please don't let him be dead already. God spare him please," I whispered under my breath, along with a couple of quick Our Fathers and Hail Marys.

With Jesse in the passenger seat, I drove his car straight to the hospital visitor's parking lot. His car is an older Honda, strikingly similar to the one I had been driving on June 10th, 1995, 25 years ago. And here we were, June 10th, 2020. I parked in the temporary lot closest to the entrance. We got out of the car, went to check in as visitors, and were told that Jesse would not be allowed into the hospital, approved visitors only. I was on the approved list.

"You'll have to stay here outside or wait in your car. You can even go home if you want and I'll be in touch. Here, put your number in my phone." It was all too much for Jesse.

"Look, I appreciate what you're trying to do, but I don't know you. And every minute I don't report this, I get in deeper. Maybe the lady I hit is still alive. I don't know what I was thinking before, but I have to call the police. I shouldn't have left. I've gotta report what happened. It's the right thing to do. The only thing to do. The police will sort it out."

"I understand, Jesse. Believe me. I get it. Go ahead and call the police if you think that's best. Just know you did not commit a crime. There was no accident. You did not hit anyone… and neither did I."

"What does that mean?" He called after me, as I turned to leave, but I couldn't explain, even if I wanted to. I needed to see the Sergeant.

With that, I left Jesse. I entered the lobby where I had my temperature checked and was asked a series of questions to ensure I would not bring the virus into the hospital. They were being careful and precautious but were not excluding visitors entirely, as I knew some other facilities were. Troy listed me as a family member, and I was grateful for that. I was fitted with a mask and paper gown. I rubbed my hands with sanitizing gel and was directed up to the eighth floor, Intensive Care unit. Sergeant Douglas Kerigan was hooked up to an IV and had a thin breathing tube inserted into his nose. His gown was open at the front and I could see wisps of thin white chest hair. The machine connected to him by stickers and wires made gentle regular beeps and I stared at the line, forming little upward triangles with every beat of the old man's frail heart. I laid my hand on his in a moment of tenderness and his eyes fluttered open and strained to focus. I felt the fragile bones in his hand, a skeleton covered in translucent skin.

"Is that you David? Look, you don't have to protect me anymore," the old man croaked. "No, Sergeant, it's me, Duncan, not David. You know, your Checkers opponent."

"Well, I need to see David. Is he here? Can you get him?"

Don't upset him, I thought. "I don't know…" I began as Troy entered the room holding the arm of an older dark-haired woman. Both wore masks and paper surgical coverups. "Duncan, this is my mom, Marcy."

"It's nice to meet you, Duncan. I'm sorry this is the occasion, though. You'll understand I can't shake your hand."

"Of course," I replied, resentful that a virus was making so many awkward situations even more difficult.

She approached the bed, and I stepped aside to make room. She leaned down close to her father. "Hi Dad. It's me, Marcy."

"Yes, yes, Marcy, my daughter…" he paused as tears leaked from the corners of his eyes. "I'm grateful you came. I don't deserve it."

This was definitely not a side of the Sergeant I'd ever

encountered.

Marcy responded, "Dad, I forgave you long ago. It was the only way I could live my life peacefully. I just wish Mom would contact me. She left us so long ago and I just can't..." She sighed deeply before continuing. "You probably don't know, but Mom and I were planning to leave together. She promised me many times, but then she'd back out. So when I was a senior in high school, I applied to colleges on my own and secured my own loans with the help of my college counselor. Mom was devastated when I broke the news, and I resented her for it. I mean, why couldn't she be happy for me? I promised to come home after graduation, but she didn't wait for me. She needed to leave that badly. Then she never called. She never forgave me. I was sure she would. It took years of therapy to get past it, Dad. You don't understand the damage you did." She sighed, "But it's over. It's in the past." It was obvious she'd rehearsed this speech many times. She stood up straighter and squared her shoulders. After a few seconds of silence, she added, "How are you doing, Dad? You Ok?"

The old man struggled to prop himself up. Troy moved to push the button on the control, allowing him to come to a seated upright position. His pallor was so gray and I thought he must not have much time left. He did not directly respond to his daughter's admission. Instead, he repeated, "Please, get David. Bring him here. I need to explain." There was a desperate, begging edge to his request.

"Grandpa, we don't know how to find David. I'm sorry. If he goes to The Regency though, they'll tell him what happened and where you are. Then he'll come. I'm sure he'll come." Troy was doing his best to reassure rather than upset his grandfather.

I felt out of place, as if I was intruding on a private family moment I had no part in, but I had to ask. "Marcy, do you happen to have a photo of your mom?" Marcy looked at me oddly, but nevertheless unzipped her purse and fished out her wallet.

"Troy told me you may have learned something from Dad." She handed me a photo. It was a square 4x4, and the white border was yellowing. The photo was taken close up and the woman's head and shoulders took up the entire frame. I flipped it over. 1985 was written in blue ink. I took my phone from my pocket.

"May I?" Marcy nodded, and I snapped a quick photo with my phone.

"Here, I've got this one too." She passed me a second photo that had been folded in half. In this one, I could see Trudy Kerigan's whole body, except her right arm, which was folded with the crease.

"You can unfold it," she said. "Dad's in the other half." When I saw the complete picture, I saw a younger, but still stern version of the Sergeant. His arm was looped with his wife and slung over his other arm was a yellow jacket. On the back, 1985. I forgot to breathe for a minute.

"Let me see those pictures," the old man called from his bed. I handed the photos to him. "Oh, my Trudy. There she is. Beautiful as ever." His eyes filled again.

"Sergeant, what's that over your arm in the photo?" I asked.

"That's my fisherman's coat, of course, my yellow slicker. Isn't it obvious?" His usual crusty personality showing itself, "Trudy liked to wear it, she did. She was wearing it when…" He gasped and one of the machines began to beep loudly. A nurse rushed in.

"Everyone needs to get out. Now." She commanded. We

hurried into the corridor. Next, we saw a doctor enter the room. And I heard, "We need to stabilize him," as the door closed.

Knowing there was nothing I could do for the Sergeant, and hoping he wouldn't pass away just yet, I stepped aside and called Jesse. His phone rang three times, then he picked up. "Hello. Duncan?"

"Yes, it's me. Where are you?"

"I'm actually still downstairs. I think I'm in shock, or this is a dream. Maybe the pot I smoked earlier was laced with something. I don't know."

"Hold on. I'll be right down. I have something to show you." I hung up and took the stairs to the first floor as fast as I could.

I didn't want Jesse to have second thoughts and leave. He sounded very shaken. I burst through the front doors, tearing off my mask and gown and stuffing them into the garbage can. I'd need fresh gear anyway if I was allowed back in. I glanced around and didn't see Jesse. My phone vibrated in my pocket. "It's me. I moved the car. Come over to the parking structure. I'm on the first floor. I'm in my car."

I ran. His old rusty Honda was in the second row. I opened the passenger side door and slid in. The crank window was already partially rolled down.

Jesse was visibly shaken. He looked worse than before when I had first picked him up. I pulled out my phone and found the two pictures I'd taken of Trudy Kerigan.

"Here, look." I thrust the screen toward him and showed him the second photo first.

"Oh, my God. That's her. That's the woman I hit. I'm sure of it. One hundred percent. That jacket. She wore that jacket, the yellow jacket. I know it's hot, it's summer, but she was wearing it." Jesse was truly distraught, and I wanted to help. I knew the feeling all too well. It had been a regular visitor, dogging me, taunting me, for 25 years. "I am so confused right now. Please explain what the hell is happening. Help me," he pleaded.

"Ok, so I can't really explain it logically, Jesse, and you probably won't believe me, but that is the same woman I hit with my car 25 years ago. The very same." I let that sink in. "This picture was taken in 1985. And the woman you see here, Trudy Kerigan, left her family that year and never returned. She was never heard from."

"So, what are you getting at?"

"I believe she was killed, hit by a car, or maybe jumped off the cliff where you and I both saw her. I think she died there, in 1985, and never left."

"So she's like a ghost or spirit or something?" He looked incredulous, but also a little relieved. "I don't believe in that sort of thing though."

"Yeah, well, neither do I, but it's the only explanation that makes sense."

He turned to me and said, "Did you see the police car pull up? I called 911 right after you went into the hospital. They came right away. I said it was an emergency, that I was involved in a hit and run."

"I don't get it. Why are you here sitting in your car? Did you hide? Are they looking for you?" I was thoroughly confused.

"No, this is where you'll have to suspend your own disbelief."

"Ok, I'm listening." I had no clue what to expect.

He continued. "The cop arrived really quickly. It seemed like less than five minutes. I actually considered taking off, making a run for it, but I'd already said I was guilty and had fled the scene of an accident. I'd already confessed to a crime. So the cop introduced himself and asked me what was going on. I started explaining what happened. How I couldn't see with the sun in my eyes. How I was driving up on Ocean View in the Upper Village, and he said, 'Let me stop you right there, Son. Who put you up to this?' I told him I didn't know what he meant, and he was like, 'Look. I don't know if this is some kind of frat boy dare or what, but I will charge you for wasting my time and this department's resources. This little scenario is getting old.' I was super confused and didn't know what to say."

"What was he talking about?" I asked.

"That's what I wanted to know. I didn't even know how to respond. I started wondering if I was in the world's strangest dream. I assured him I had no clue what he meant. At this point, I was losing it. I was crying and sweating and shaking. I sat down on the pavement, afraid I'd pass out or vomit right there. He must have realized I wasn't messing around. He told me his department gets at least a couple calls a year about that place. Someone phones in and confesses to a fake hit-and-run. Police come out, take a look, take a report and nothing comes of it. Nothing. No evidence, no body. No witnesses. He even mentioned the exact location, and the tree that grows there. He thinks it's some kind of years-long ongoing prank. He was surprised I gave my real name and location. He said most of the time it's an 'anonymous' tip about a hit and run, usually in summer, always the same location."

"So others have seen it too," I said. "I wonder how many of us there are, and why we haven't heard of it? You'd think it'd be in the papers or on the news."

"I think the police want to keep it quiet, or there might be even more false reports and copycats," Jesse replied.

"Well, all I know is that bit of knowledge would have saved me years of self-torture and guilt."

I told Jesse to go home. Even though we had just met, I felt like I knew the kid. I said to keep my number. I'd be happy to help him find a job. He reminds me so much of myself at that age. I made a quick call to Julia, letting her know I needed more time, but everything was okay with Jesse. The police cleared him and there was no accident. She was relieved. I let her know I was visiting Sergeant Kerigan in the hospital and would Uber home if it got too late. As close as Julia and I are, I have never shared my deep, dark secret with her. I came close a few times, but ultimately decided against it. Why should she have to fight my demons? I've perfected masking my distress and guilt.

At this point, I was certain I had not killed anyone, but I was disappointed that the sense of relief I expected was not there. I still had questions. Still felt confused. If the accident wasn't real, what about my persistent feeling of being watched? What about the other strange occurrences? I was not fully convinced someone, or something, was not out to harm me. Maybe Trudy's spirit, if that's what it was, had somehow attached itself to me.

I hung up with Julia and my phone vibrated. It was Troy. "Hey, Grandpa's stabilized. You can come back up." I told Troy I'd need to sign back in and suit up and I'd see him in a few. The administrator was talking to a guy in the line. I overheard their conversation.

"Yes, I'm on the list. He'll want to see me. I'm his only friend. David. David Miller." The check-in nurse gave the man a disdainful once over, but then checked the list and confirmed he was on it.

She handed him a paper head cover, mask, gown, foot covers and a pass, saying, "You need to put this protective gear on and wash your hands as well as sanitize them. We have very ill people here."

His graying brown hair was greasy and longer in the back, hanging limply over his flannel shirt collar. The arms were cut off at the shoulders, making what Dad liked to call a "redneck tank top." His jeans were ragged and filthy. So were his fully visible feet with yellowed toenails and calloused heels in worn-out flip-flops. He stepped aside to suit up. I re-checked in and was handed my own protective gear. I dressed quickly and made my way to the elevator. I pushed the call button and waited. When the door slid open, I stepped inside and was joined by the man from the line. I pushed the button for eight and I stared straight ahead, uninterested in making light conversation, but I could feel his eyes on me. Then he tapped my shoulder to get my attention. I cringed.

"Hey, I know you," he said.

"No, I don't think so," I replied without making eye contact.

"Aren't you going to see the Sergeant?"

"Yes."

"Well, so am I. He's a friend of mine."

This must be David. The guy the Sergeant was asking for. I inspected him, and he seemed a little familiar, but all I could really see were his eyes. His head, mouth and nose were covered in paper hospital protective gear. How would I know this guy? When would we have met? Still, something about his voice shook me. His presence was unnerving, and I was relieved when the elevator opened at the fourth floor and two more people stepped in. David did not try to continue the conversation. We both got out on the eighth floor and proceeded to the Sergeant's room. I hung back, wanting to put space between us. Then it hit me. Wasn't this the guy who all but accosted me at Dad's funeral?

Troy and Marcy were standing outside the room when we walked over and I thought the worst; the Sergeant had died. Troy said his grandfather had asked for a priest and he was speaking to one now. I could only imagine how that conversation was going. Troy acknowledged David, saying, "Hi, it's been a long time. It was nice of you to come. My Grandpa has been asking for you."

David answered, "It's the least I could do. I'm his only real friend." David stared at me while speaking to Troy. It was unnerving, and I wondered what his problem was. The conversation did not go further. We stood in silence, checking our phones to look busy and to avoid stilted conversation.

Soon the priest came out with his head bowed and his hands folded and clasping a rosary, and again, we all privately thought the worst. But the priest motioned for us to go into the room, saying, "Mr. Kerigan will see you now. Please let him speak without judgment. He hasn't much time left."

Though it was technically against the rules, the nurse on duty allowed us all into the room together, Marcy, Troy, Me, and David. David and I hung back near the foot of the bed. I wasn't comfortable being in such close proximity to him, but the room was small and there was no way to put more distance between us. Marcy pulled the only chair close to her father, and Troy stood behind his mother. The Sergeant's eyes were shut, his hands folded high on his chest. He could have been in a casket posed for family and friends to pay their respects. Marcy spoke first, "Dad, I'm here, and I want to make things right with you. There's not much time."

His eyes fluttered open, and he gazed at his daughter. "Marcy, I've waited far too long to say this and I don't deserve your understanding or forgiveness, but I'm asking for it." He took a deep breath and related his truth. "I was mean, Marcy. I know it. And a terrible husband to your mother. I was jealous."

"You were, Dad. You were," Marcy agreed.

"Every time I went out on the fishing boat and came back, I accused her of cheating on me. I had no reason to suspect her. She did nothing to deserve it, except being so beautiful and being too good for me. When I was a boy, my mother constantly told me I was ugly and stupid. She raised me alone and blamed me for ruining her life and her body just by being born. I took off as soon as I was old enough and joined the Army and in four years, earned my rank of Sergeant and when my time was up, I didn't re-enlist. My civilian life began. I met your mom and we married right away, but I never knew how to be a proper husband. I worked hard on the fishing boats after leaving the Army. A couple of my buddies and I bought a boat, and we did well. Then bought two more. We started doing charter trips for hobby fishermen and we made great money. That's how I bought the house. It was cheap then, compared to now. I'm glad I'll have something to leave you, Marcy. Maybe you'll be able to forgive me someday." He sighed and reached for a glass of water. Troy handed it to him and he took a sip, then sunk back into his pillow. He looked worn out. *Was that it?* We waited expectantly.

"Dad. Please. Do you know where Mom is?" Marcy begged again. Then he continued his confession. At least it felt like a confession to me. I had never heard him speak with such clarity and wondered if he really had dementia, or if it had been a ruse all along.

"You always thought your mom left you, but she didn't. She left me. When you went to college and there were just the two of us, we fought all the time. It was miserable. She finally said she was leaving and would send me the papers for a divorce. She was done with me." He wrung his hands together, then pushed back what remained of his hair. Again, we waited.

"Please, Dad, go on."

"Well, I couldn't take it. I begged her not to leave. She wouldn't listen. I forced her back into the house. I grabbed a knife. And stabbed her tires. So she couldn't drive away." The Sergeant was growing more agitated, speaking in starts and stops. "The knife was to show her I was serious." He stopped speaking again and let out a groan. "I never meant to hurt her at all. I pulled the phone from the wall. I didn't want her to call anyone." The old man paused again, then muttered, "No one's damn business." It was torture, waiting for him to just get the words out.

"Back then, there were only a few other properties up on the mountain nearby. There wasn't anywhere for her to go. I apologized. She unpacked her bag. Said she'd stay. I was gonna make things right. I said I'd go to church, start over, whatever she wanted. She said, 'Sure, Dougie.' That's what she called me when things were good between us, 'whatever you want.' Then I started drinking. That was my mistake. And things got ugly again that same evening."

I looked over at Marcy and saw that she was crying. So was Troy. He moved closer to his mother and put his arm more firmly around her. "Dad, what happened to Mom? Where is she?" Marcy pleaded.

217

"She's gone." His tone was abrupt, followed by silence. We all held our breath.

"Dad. Please."

"Trudy left that night, on foot. It was the only way. She took one of my yellow fisherman jackets and just walked out. With nothing else. She wanted to escape me." He was crying now. "When I figured out she was gone, I got in my truck. Just to go after her. To bring her back. I swear to you, Marcy, I wanted to bring her back home. I wanted to work things out. I drove down the mountain. Looking for her. I saw her walking on the side of the road, saw that bright yellow jacket, and then she saw me." The old man looked at Marcy. "I can't, Marcy. I can't," he said.

"You have to Dad. Tell me what happened!" She was frantic.

"Well, she crossed in front of the truck. And, and I, I hit her, Marcy. I hit her with the car. It was an accident."

The old man's voice rose in frantic volume as the memory fully enveloped him. He drew a sharp breath in, and looked at Marcy and Troy before casting his eyes down and dropping his voice. We stood in shock, no one able to speak, watching the Sergeant remember the night.

"It was a curvy part of the road. You know how dangerous Ocean View is, how there's the cliff-side. There wasn't even a guardrail back then. They put that up later. I called out to her. She didn't answer. It was after one in the morning. Pitch black. I didn't have my flashlight."

Marcy interrupted, "Dad! You killed her! You killed Mom and just left her? How, how could you do that?" His voice dropped to an even lower level, hardly a whisper as he attempted to rationalize.

"Well, now I never did know if she was dead or not. I

still thought maybe she just went away. Maybe none of that happened. I'd been drinking a lot that night. I blacked out. I might've dreamt it. I had a real problem then. You know, she may have just left. I did a search the next morning. Well, it was afternoon once I got up. I didn't see anything. Figured I imagined the whole thing. Figured she'd call me when she got wherever she was headed. But she didn't call. She never did call. And you know what? I think I may have killed her that night."

His eyes looked distant as he said it. His shoulders slumped in relief after unloading his burden. All of us were frozen. We just stood in silent shock over what we'd just heard, perfectly and clearly from a man who had suffered from dementia for the last five years at least.

Then the man, David, spoke up. "Why'd you say that, Sergeant? Now you'll go to jail for murder. They'll probably call the sheriff right away. Your secret was safe. You know I'd never tell. Never. I had your back. It wasn't you that killed her, it was this guy." And he pointed his dirty finger in my face.

"What the hell are you talking about? You're crazy! And don't point your finger at me!"

He pulled down his paper face mask and got right up close and I was assaulted by the smell of damp earth and the feel of his breath in my face. Anger surged in my body and I wanted to shove him with both hands, but somehow I refrained, realizing how completely inappropriate that would be in a dying man's hospital room. Everything was happening too fast.

"You are the killer!" He shouted. Then he lowered his voice and continued speaking, but the words he spoke were not his, but mine. Words straight out of my journal. My private thoughts being spat back at me in front of others.

"It was the third curvy turn. I hit a woman in a yellow jacket. It was 1:35 AM June 10, 1995. Saturday night after four beers and two jello shots. Shall I continue?" David asked. Then he said, "You know me."

All at once, images from the past clicked. I remembered. The transient outside of the thrift store years ago, the homeless man in the church, the criminal at the Government Center. And that smell.

"You've been in my house!" I accused him.

"Yes. Many times," he said coolly.

"But why? And how? Who are you and what do you want with me?"

"You still don't know, Duncan? You always only cared about yourself. You probably never thought about me again after 6th grade."

"6th grade?" I was baffled. What was he talking about?

"It's me Barty. Barton Miller."

"It can't be you. I heard you were dead. I cried for you. I felt bad about our childhood, how I wasn't nice to you. How I didn't want you to come over. How I resented you."

"That's rich. You resent me. Yours was the only genuine friendship I ever had when I was a kid. Your parents were the only ones who ever treated me kindly. Your mom still does. Why do you think I show up almost every day at Helping Hands? Why do you think I went to your father's funeral? Yes, that was me. I've seen you so many times over the years. I tried to remind you who I was, and every time you denied me. Pretended not to know me. You made me feel less than human. I kept giving you chances to repent, but you wouldn't. So I took my revenge and continued to torture you all these years."

"But Barton Miller died," I repeated quietly. "I don't know who you are."

"I didn't die. When I was 18, I changed my name to David. I wanted a new identity."

"Then who was the man the sheriff said was Barton Miller?"

"Some other homeless man. Some of my friends and I said his name was Barton Miller to mess with the cops. I came up with the name so I could officially be dead as Barty. The cops eventually figured out who the dead guy really was, I'm sure. Or maybe not. For all I know, they never checked it out. You can certainly confirm that all homeless people look alike, right? Can't tell one from the next."

He was throwing the fact I'd written him out of my life and never looked back in my face.

"So if I would have recognized you and acknowledged you, you wouldn't have tortured me all these years?"

"Probably not. The Sergeant needed his secret kept, and I knew from spying on you that you, too, had a secret, so it worked out well, especially when the bones were found in 2010."

"Bones?" Marcy said meekly. I'd forgotten where we were for a minute and was thrust back into reality, into the hospital room of a dying man. A dying man who had callously murdered his wife.

"Um, yes. There were bones found when Ocean View Drive was being graded and they were shoring up the hillside. They were determined to be the remains of a woman in her 50s and the bones were at least 20-25 years old..." I trailed off, not wanting to make the conclusion.

"Oh my God! Mom!" Marcy broke down, "I always thought about it. I knew she would have called me. But I

221

just didn't want to accept it."

"Now you know," David said with what almost sounded like a little tenderness.

2021

T HE SERGEANT DIED TWO weeks later, after quietly slip-
ping into a coma the same night of his confession. I
think he said what he needed to say, got it all off his chest,
and could finally be at peace. The revelation shocked Marcy
and Troy, but it provided needed closure, too. We shared the
information with Sheriff Shiloh, who agreed to keep it quiet.
There was no need for publicity. Through DNA analysis,
the bones found in 2010 were officially identified as those of
Trudy Kerigan and were properly laid to rest by her daughter,
Marcy, and grandson, Troy.

I sat down with Julia and my mom and finally told them
everything, apologizing profusely for not being honest.
They were supportive and understanding and only wished
I hadn't suffered alone for so many years.

David, "Barty" Miller agreed, albeit with reluctance, to
take part in a rehab program for drug addiction. Over the
years, he had been in and out of permanent housing and had
tried many times to get and stay drug free. My mom, whom
he trusted, helped him get into transitional housing and job

training after I paid for the rehab program. I don't want him to know, but I will see to it that he will never be homeless again. I prefer not to have any contact directly with him yet, but I wish the best for him and want to provide him the opportunity to live a decent life.

Everyone deserves that. Forgiving him was easier than I imagined. I was incredibly relieved to know I was innocent and not crazy. So now I begin the next 25 years of my life with a clean slate and a new appreciation for living the truth.

About Author

Deanna Nese is the author of two other novels. *Shelter in Place* (2014) is a contemporary Christian fiction tale of three women coming together to help a young mother raise her child. *The Needle's Eye* (2016) is a young adult fantasy fiction story with excellent reviews from Kirkus and Reader's Choice. Her short story, *Frank's Reviews* was published by Typishly in 2018. Her flash fiction has been published in the VC Reporter.

She teaches middle school students English Literature, Writing, and History. She enjoys outdoor activities, reading and writing in all genres, and spending time with her family.

Acknowledgments

Writing a novel is a long, sometimes lonely, and trying process. No one knows this better than fellow writers. I'd like to thank my writing group, Dr. Phyllisann Maguire, Lori Iori, and Melinda Belcher. Our monthly meetings and their willingness to give me encouraging feedback, as well as allowing me to read their works-in-progress, really helped me move forward.

Thank you, Shirley O'Neil Robertson and Phyllisann Maguire for being there for the whole process and getting to know these characters as they developed. Your candid feedback, friendship, loyalty, and support is invaluable.

Thank you to my beta readers: Philip Barbaro, Chris Dunmire, and Dr. Colleen Robertson, your insight was very much appreciated.

Thank you to my best friend Trisha Gazin, my biggest cheerleader, who is always there for me through thick and thin, and has been since we were three.

Thank you to Green Avenue Books and Publishing for believing in this story and getting it on the shelves and into the hands of readers.